KING OF NOTHING

KINGMAKER TRILOGY
BOOK 1

PAULA DOMBROWIAK

KINGMAKER BOOK ONE

KING OF *Nothing*

PAULA DOMBROWIAK

KING of Nothing

By: Paula Dombrowiak
Copyright © 2024 Paula Dombrowiak

All rights reserved. No part of this publication may be reproduced, stored in any retrieval system, or transmitted in any form or by any means, including electronic, mechanical, photocopy, recording, or otherwise, without the prior written permission of the above copyright owner of this book.

This is a work of fiction. Names, characters, places, brands, media, and incidents are either the products of the author's imagination or are used fictitiously.

Cover Image: Stock Photo's
Cover Design: Paula Dombrowiak
Editor: Hart to Heart Edits
Proofreader: Katy Nielsen

www.pauladombrowiak.com

CONTENTS

1. The Game Begins — 1
2. Frivolous Matters — 11
3. Heart of Gold — 25
4. The Kingmaker — 37
5. Pretty Girl Like You — 51
6. Less is More — 57
7. Bluebloods Run Cold — 61
8. Dainty Waist for a Man — 71
9. Elvis Tribute Package — 81
10. Paris Syndrome — 87
11. Queenie — 95
12. Give All to Love — 103
13. Georgetown T-Shirt — 115
14. Souvenir from Vegas — 121
15. My Wife — 129
16. Grief, Revenge, Spite — 139
17. Get your Own — 147
18. You Don't Marry Them — 153
19. Squirrel — 161
20. Dog and Pony Show — 165
21. Emerson — 181
22. I Don't Belong to You — 187
23. How A Bill Becomes A Law — 195
24. You Taught Me Well — 201
25. The Perfect Fuck You — 205

    Queen of Ruin Excerpt — 215

Also by Paula Dombrowiak — 219
About the Author — 221
Acknowledgments — 223

For Poopsie, our brainstorming session is what led to Darren and Evangeline's story.

1
The Game Begins

Evangeline

I place my clutch on the top of the dark mahogany bar and take a seat, crossing one leg over the other, facing the opulent chandelier that hangs from the ceiling. The crystals send prisms of light to dance on the walls, giving the space a beautiful touch of color. With no windows to let in the early evening light, the space is otherwise dark, like deep waters. The upscale bar is decorated with plush couches in a deep shade of pink, fluffy pillows, and shadowy corners. In a town like Las Vegas, this bar is an oasis for those who want to be anonymous—and have enough money to pay for it.

I grab the bartender's attention, his eyes lingering on my face for only a second before they fall to the low cut of my dress. He offers me an embarrassed smile when he notices that I've caught him staring at the outline of my breasts.

I don't mind.

Otherwise, I wouldn't be wearing a dress that leaves so little to the imagination.

He's young and handsome, nicely built, with a kind smile, and a great head of hair which I'm sure helps with the tips. His uniform of a crisp white dress shirt and black vest are neatly pressed. The glint of a gold name tag pinned to the lapel reads Tony.

"Champagne?"

I have to order something while I'm here waiting. I typically don't drink, not because I can't handle my liquor, but I need to have a clear head. That's why only one glass of champagne is my limit.

Tony knows *who* I am, or more importantly, *what* I am.

The glass appears in front of me and I hold it by the stem, letting the last of the foam fizz out before taking a sip, leaving behind an imprint of red lipstick.

Across the room, I see a man walking towards me in a very expensive dark suit with a bold blue tie. He's tall, distinguished, with a head of dark hair that is now peppered with grey. He's handsome, but that hardly matters. He makes his way over with an interested smile. He takes the seat next to me at the bar and I swallow hard, giving him a practiced smile because that's what I'm supposed to do, when everything inside of me wants to get up from this chair and walk out the door.

"Hello," he says in a confident, smooth voice.

There is no indication in his demeanor that we have met before, but his eyes glint with recognition and unrequited want.

And so the game begins. "Hello."

"Are you here for the conference?" he asks, resting his arm on top of the bar, his fingers close to my arm as if itching to touch me.

I look down at my dress, cut low, cinched at the waist, and flaring out at just the right length to show off my legs which his eyes drop further down to admire.

The music and the chatter in the bar aren't loud, but I lean in anyway, my lips close to his ear, giving him a decent view down the front of my dress, and ask, "Do I look like I'm here for a conference?"

I can hear the long intake of breath as if he's admiring my perfume, and when I straighten, I notice the flare of his nostrils and the black pupils of his eyes swallowing up the pale blue.

"No, I don't suppose you are." His laugh is deep, but not the nervous laugh of a man who is embarrassed or shy talking to a beautiful woman. It's the practiced laugh of a politician.

He scans my face, taking in my wheat-colored hair that hangs in waves to just below my collarbone, and his eyes settle on my plump red lips. I blink, and he pushes a few stray pieces of my bangs away from my eyes as if to see me better.

I let him, because after all, he did pay for me.

My job is to tempt men into thinking I'm obtainable when neither of us have the intention of more than just one night. It's the illusion they pay for, and a heavy payment at that. He's already paid for it, so I know he wants to fuck me – that's why he asked specifically for me, and my heart beats against my chest at the thought.

"I'd ask to buy you a drink, but I see you already have one," he says in a smooth tone, pointing to the champagne flute in front of me, his gold cufflinks reflecting light from the chandelier.

I catch Tony's eye and signal for the check with a flick of my wrist.

Turning my attention back to the man next to me, I ask, "So, what brings you to Vegas?" I hold the glass to my lips, taking a sip, feeling the bubbles pop on my tongue while he watches ever so intently.

He smiles, sitting straighter in his chair, clearly liking this game very much. "Business."

Business, indeed.

Tony slides the billfold purposefully towards the man and nods at me before leaving.

"What's your name?" he asks, keeping up the pretense that we've never met. He looks at the lipstick left behind on my glass, and by the glimmer in his eye and the way he shifts in his seat, I can safely say that he's imagining that lipstick mark around his cock.

I wonder how long he's thought about me.

"Holly," I answer, because *tonight,* that's who I am.

"Holly." He swirls my name around with his tongue like he's tasting a fine wine. "I like that."

He tucks a few bills, including a nice tip, into the billfold, his eyes never leaving mine.

He doesn't wait for me to ask his name, but of course I already know it. I know a lot about him... Things I don't want to know.

"Jonathan," he introduces himself.

His eyes blanket me with a satisfied expression. Before holding out his arm for me to take, he asks, "Do you have any idea how long I have waited for this?" His mouth tilts into a pleased smile.

I know exactly how long he's been waiting: four years.

I slide off the seat, my stilettos planted firmly on the ornate carpet beneath me. "So, Senator?" I take his arm graciously and then grab my clutch from the bar top. "What would you like to do with me?" I ask with a smile.

"What are you going to school for?" Elsie, the elderly woman sitting across from me, asks. Her wrist is adorned with the most beautiful bracelets that tinkle together when she lifts her arm. On her finger is a vintage ring with a large, single diamond at its center. Everything about her screams poise and wealth.

She was introduced to me as the wife of a lobbyist for The National Association of Realtors. Her husband, Otto Reynolds, is in deep conversation with my date, Senator Jonathan Langley.

"Literature," I answer naturally, taking a bite of my salmon, which is quite flavorful. A glass of red wine sits in front of me, untouched.

"What kind of job will you get with a degree in literature?" She laughs in the condescending way women of her era laugh without meaning to. It's just part of her upbringing – to look down on girls like me who have this romanticism about life instead of being practical and entering a respectable career path until I marry a judge or a lobbyist and start having babies.

I sit up straighter, setting my utensil next to my half-eaten plate of food. "Do you remember Melinda Carleton?"

She pinches her brows together as the cogs in her mind turn, trying to place the name.

"The woman who won a Pulitzer for the story she wrote for *The Post* about confidential military papers being leaked to Russian spies," I refresh her memory, and Elsie's face opens up in recognition. Everyone remembers that story, it brought down a high White House official. Elsie nods, seeming impressed that I would be so informed about political matters.

"She has a degree in literature," I explain, picking up my glass of water and taking a sip.

Her mouth forms the shape of an 'O', but no sound comes out, having been put in her place, and I should feel satisfied, but I don't... Because I'm *not* a literature student, not anymore. I will never write a story like Melinda Carleton did for *The Post*, or any other paper for that matter.

I'm an escort to the rich and powerful – to men who need discretion. Because if they were found with someone like me, their political career would be over, and I have no intention of having my picture all over the news or bringing attention to the exclusive agency I'm with. To say that Ellen would not be happy would be an understatement.

I'd never work again.

I'm playing a game right now, introduced as a friend of the family, and I mingle as if I'm one of them, as if I will move on to do great things because of my stellar upbringing and family money. But once dinner is over, and for a hefty price, I'll be taken to a hotel room where Senator Langley will be able to live out the fantasy he's had for the past four years.

This is the life I chose and I'm not ashamed of it, but I had other plans. These were just the cards I was dealt. So I play my part in the game because that's who these men want – the fantasy – not the real me.

In some ways I'm no different than these other women at the table, because we're all getting paid, one way or the other, to fuck their husbands. The only difference for me is that I get to leave in the morning with my money. If *they* want to leave, lawyers and prenups are involved.

"Would you like dessert?" The waiter's question interrupts my thoughts and he looks at the guests expectantly, but none are paying attention to him.

Under the table I feel Jonathan's hand on my thigh, the table linen hiding it from view. His fingers inch further up my leg and slip under the hem of my dress. The waiter stands awkwardly trying to get the attention of the table, unaware that the Senator's fingers are now gliding under my panties.

When he feels that I'm bare, a slow, satisfied smile tugs at the edges of his lips and his eyes dissolve into molten pools of blue. He looks away from me only long enough to address the waiter.

"Yes, dessert sounds good," he says, sliding his eyes back to mine as he slips a finger inside me. The pulse in his neck flutters wildly and he swallows hard as I part my lips in response.

"I'll just bring a variety for the table," the waiter says and quietly dissolves back into the darkness. The entire restaurant feels like dusk, each table only lit by elegant candles while ornate sconces line the red textured wallpaper, and when I tip my head back to look at the ceiling I don't find one, because it's decorated to look like an endless starry night.

While the other guests continue their conversations, I grip the edge of the table trying desperately to school my expression as Senator Langley's finger slowly pumps in and out of me. My clit grows more sensitive with each pass, my body betraying me—reacting because of biology rather than attraction. Every intake of my breath seems to fuel him, to know that what he's doing affects me. He thinks it gives him power over me.

I learned a long time ago that you don't have to be in love with someone to enjoy sex. Being paid to enjoy it doesn't make the orgasm spin you out of control any less than if you weren't paid. In fact, it might even be better.

Men like Senator Langley like to be in control. After all, that's the very basis of being in politics: having a hand in policies that affect millions of Americans, especially the ones that safeguard *his own* wealth. Fingering me under the table with his friends only a few feet away is all a part of his game, and I play along because that's what I'm paid to do.

His skilled fingers begin to lull me into a haze. I have to resist pumping my hips in order to chase the high and relieve the building pressure at my apex. Slowly I'm falling into submission, internally begging for his thumb to skim my clit once again, but that doesn't mean that I'm powerless. In fact, it's the other way around, because I know he's dependent on getting me off.

When the waiter returns with the plate full of desserts, all I hear are the taps of utensils against porcelain plates and the sound of ice tumbling against glasses as chatter resumes. I am close—so close that I don't care if the other prominent members of the House and their wives can hear me because my orgasm is right there, inching its way up my throat – and he can feel it.

Nearby I hear a shrill, "Oh my God!" come from the table followed by a collective gasp. My eyes snap open, and Jonathan's fingers pull out of me so suddenly that it's like a punch to the gut.

My heart hammers in my chest. I adjust my dress and settle back into my seat, but no one is looking at me or

Senator Langley, who's awkwardly adjusting himself under the table. The phone sitting next to me lights up with a news alert: *Senator Kerry Walker and wife Merrill Compton-Walker Dead in a Helicopter crash.*

My eyes widen at the news, and I instinctively place a hand to my chest as if to keep my heart in place.

Senator Kerry Walker.

My heart feels as though it has stopped in the middle of a beat, pressing against my ribcage.

"Oh dear, did you know him?" Elsie asks, and that's when I feel a tear spill over onto my cheek which I quickly wipe away with the back of my hand.

I want to say that I did know him once, that I never stopped thinking about him. But of course, I can't, especially with Jonathan sitting next to me.

I just shake my head. Jonathan clears his throat and reaches over to pick up his phone. The platter of desserts sits at the center of the table half-eaten as guests are glued to their phones while more news comes in.

"Such a shame," someone across from me says.

"Shit," Jonathan mutters, getting up from the table and throwing his napkin on the chair. He motions hurriedly for the bill as several of the guests stand, collecting their belongings as they ready to leave.

"I need to know if we can swing someone else," Jonathan says gruffly into his phone. "Yes, I'm aware," he says angrily and turns away from me, lowering his voice, but I don't care to listen to his conversation.

When the waiter returns with the bill, Senator Langley motions across the table to Otto Reynolds, who makes a face but reluctantly takes the billfold.

"Holly," Senator Langley holds his hand out to help me up.

We stand awkwardly at the entrance while other guests pass by, still voicing their condolences and shock over the news.

"Thank you for a lovely evening," I say, attempting to leave, but he grabs my arm, fingers digging into my flesh hard enough that they're sure to leave a bruise.

Jonathan's eyes rake over my body and I blink momentarily, losing myself.

"I thought…"

"I've already paid for the evening," he cuts me off, his eyes flaring.

He lets go of my arm as another guest, Marcus Wimbley, stops to shake the Senator's hand, and I can tell by Senator Langley's body language that he's annoyed at being delayed his dessert.

Marcus turns towards me with his clever brown eyes. "It was a pleasure to meet you, but we have some things to discuss."

"I will speak with you later, Marcus. I need to see Ms. Hart home safely."

"I'm afraid this cannot wait," he says sternly, "and I'm sure Ms. *Bowen* can find *herself* safely home."

He knows who I am – and he wants to make sure Senator Langley knows that he knows.

2
Frivolous Matters

Darren

"What lies before us, gentlemen…."

Alistair stands precariously on top of the pool table holding a tumbler of expensive whiskey. Behind him are floor-to-ceiling windows looking out over the blinding lights of the Las Vegas Strip, and in the distance is the gaudy replica of the Eiffel Tower.

"And what lies behind us," —he makes a point to drag out the words so they sound much more ominous then they need to be, and it has its desired effect because the chatter in the hotel suite quiets, and everyone turns their attention to him—"are but frivolous matters." He pauses for affect, a mischievous smile on his face. "Compared with what is *in* us!" he shouts victoriously, as if he's just led an army into battle instead of downing a glass of whiskey.

The room full of people—some we hardly know, and some we wish we didn't—explodes into chaotic cheers.

Someone yells, "*Dick*," and Alistair whirls around, teetering on the edge of the pool table, holding his hand flat above his eyes as he scans the crowd.

"Who goes there?" he says teasingly, right before tumbling off the edge and landing on the couch with a thud.

He's gotten the quote wrong, but Alistair was never a good student. I've known Alistair Van der Walt a long time. During our tenure as fraternity brothers, we bonded over our love of fine whiskey and fine pussy, getting as much of both as we could. Brothers in our fraternity and brothers in mischief, we'd also bonded over being the degenerate sons of Washington's upper-class. Even though we graduated years ago, we still hadn't outgrown our love of fine whiskey, but at least we'd upgraded our search for even finer pussy. Alistair's search led him to getting caught with the daughter of a judge – a judge I was clerking for. Guilty by association—and the fact that I was in his home while Alistair was defiling his daughter upstairs in her room —I was promptly and ceremoniously fired.

To avoid the disapproving look of his mother and the wrath of his father, he called me and said, "What does one do when they are at the center of a scandal?" to which I promptly replied, "Why, create another scandal." Which is how we ended up in Las Vegas.

Alistair looks up at me with his head in my lap as if he doesn't remember how he got in this position. He turns himself upright only to lean forward to cut a line of coke on the coffee table in front of him.

"Only you could quote Ralph Waldo Emerson in reference to getting high," I tease him.

"And they said we'd have no use for nineteenth

century transcendentalist poetry in the real world," Alistair laughs, flinging his head back as he inhales sharply and then settles further into the couch like a cat settling in for a nap.

"How much did your college diploma cost your father?" I take the line when he passes it to me.

When I open my eyes again, a familiar blonde stands in front of me with her perfect posture, like a debutante who was taught to balance a stack of books on her head.

We went to Georgetown law together, although she was just coming in as I was making my way out. Her family is old money, the kind that gets you into the Daughters of the American Revolution.

"Darren Walker," she says, touching my arm. "It's been a while."

I pinch my brows together, and in my head sound out the names *Miffy, Muffy*... When I don't answer right away, she gives me a reprieve. "Tiffany."

"Yes!" I point my finger in the air as if I did in fact remember her name.

She shakes her head disapprovingly but laughs it off. "We had Constitutional Law together," she goes on to explain. "Your debate on the Fourteenth Amendment was legendary," she says this time with an approving smile.

"Ah, yes," I say, tipping back the contents of my glass, draining the last of the whiskey.

"So what firm did you pick?"

"None," I say. I'd only gone to law school to appease my father and make my mother happy, but I had no intentions of working eighty hours a week at some stuffy firm.

"None?" she blanches. "I thought since…"

"What brings you here, Tiffany?"

I can only assume she's taken a position at a prestigious firm as a junior associate with a plush office in a high rise overlooking the Hudson—that is until she marries one of the partners and pops out a few babies, because that's what girls like her do.

"I guess I wanted to blow off some steam," she laughs nervously.

I smirk, pushing a few stray hairs off my forehead as I sweep my eyes down her body.

"And blow off steam you will."

Standing to my full height, I dip my head to meet her eyes. I have nothing but time and money, and there is nothing better than wasting both on a beautiful blonde. When I lean in to kiss her, she presses a hand to my chest, and with wide eyes, looks around me and asks, "Isn't that your father?"

I turn around, annoyed, expecting to find my father standing behind me, but he wasn't there. Instead, he was on the TV. I didn't want to watch a fucking news segment about my father, especially not while I'm high and trying to get laid.

"Who turned on the fucking news?" I yell, annoyed.

Alistair grabs the remote from the table presumably to turn it off, but as I stare at the TV, the scene causes me to hold up my palm to stop him.

The newscaster's voice cuts through the noise of the room, sharp and somber, and it causes a chill to run up my spine.

Kerry Walker, the enigmatic Senator from Virginia and his wife, Merrill Compton-Walker, were killed in a helicopter crash this evening on their way back to Washington D.C from their home in Southern Virginia. The helicopter experienced mechanical failure upon takeoff. A full investigation is underway.

I can hear the collective gasp just before the room goes silent which amplifies the newscaster's stiff voice. The phone in my pocket vibrates. Dexter Rausch, my father's chief of staff, is displayed on the screen. I clutch the phone so tight I think the screen might break, but I don't answer it. I didn't like speaking to Dexter before, and I certainly don't want to speak to him now.

The newscaster goes on to talk about Kerry Walker as if he knows him, speaking of his strong sense of justice because of his humble upbringing, but he doesn't know anything about the real Kerry Walker. He doesn't know Kerry Walker, *the father* or Kerry Walker, *the husband.*

All I can hear is the blood pumping in my ears as I watch the TV, the visuals of the crash site now imprinted in my mind, and yet it feels as though I'm watching a movie and not real life.

"Dare?" Alistair's voice is close to a whisper as he places a hand on my shoulder. The weight of it feels heavy and foreign as I'm brought out of my thoughts and back to reality – back to the blaring TV as the newscaster continues on about my father's career.

"One sentence." I hold up a finger to him in anger, but it's not him I'm angry with.

Alistair shakes his head in confusion.

"They couldn't give my mother more than just one sentence."

"I think – I think you're in shock."

Spinning around the room, I notice everyone staring at me, their mouths open, eyes wide, waiting for what I'm going to do or say. I feel like a fish in a fishbowl.

"Get out!" I roar, but I only gain the attention of those within earshot, because the rest of them seem to be swallowed up by the TV.

"Dare, come on." Alistair grabs my arm, trying to calm me down. "You need to go home."

Home? Where the fuck is home?

I turn to Alistair and I hate the way he's looking at me. He's never serious. He's the guy you get high with, pick up girls with, stand on top of a pool table and quote Emerson with—not the voice of reason. "If they won't fucking leave, I will." I shake off his hand and push my way through the crowd of shocked and confused faces.

The phone in my back pocket vibrates relentlessly, and I pull it out again to see Rausch's name on the screen.

I stare at the phone as I wait impatiently for the private elevator doors to open, aware of everyone's eyes on my back. I can still hear the television in the background, which is now the loudest sound in the room.

Kerry and Merrill Walker, who met in law school, married six months later, lived in a one-bedroom apartment around the corner from the non-profit Kerry worked at to support a wife who was then pregnant—

With me.

The phone in my hand continues to vibrate, and the screen lights up with too many text messages to comprehend. I don't even remember the elevator ride down, but the minute I exit into the crowded casino, I drop the phone in the nearest garbage can, glad to be rid of it.

There's something I need at this moment, more than my phone – more than I need to breathe.

"I'M SORRY, I'm not allowed to serve you any more."

Behind the bartender is a glass wall reflecting light from the chandelier that hangs in the center of the room. Luckily, I can't see my reflection through the bottles of liquor—not that it would deter me from demanding another drink.

The bartender doesn't look like he's budging, so I dig into my pocket and pull out a few hundred-dollar bills, slapping them ceremoniously in front of him with the same pointed look he's giving me. Some scholars might argue that math is the universal language, but I would beg to differ and say that it's money.

Squinting, I try to make out the name tag on the lapel of his black vest. Slowly, the letters line up. "Another shot, *Tony*," I demand.

He shakes his head with a disgusted look as he pushes the bills back towards me. "Not gonna lose my job for some overprivileged drunk who's just gonna go home to his penthouse."

"Are you discriminating against the rich?" I ask, slurring my words. "I think there are laws against that." I search my brain to remember discriminatory law, but everything I learned in law school is currently swimming in whiskey.

Tony stands to his full height, folding his arms across his chest. "I'll ask you nicely to leave, but if I have to ask again, it won't be nice."

Laughing, I gather the money and try to get up from my stool, but gravity has other plans. As the room spins and my judgment clouds even more, there is one thing that becomes clear in my mind... a single thought that has plagued me since I saw the news about my parents.

The framed poem that hangs in my father's office

behind his chair – the "Boston Hymn," his favorite of Emerson's. I would stare at it while being lectured. *Good looks and money will only get you so far in life*, he would say to me, and I would tune out the rest because it didn't matter. I was still going to be the degenerate son of Senator Walker, the son he had to hold press conferences about and explain my indiscretions to the media.

And my mother. My mother, Merrill Compton-Walker...

You could do so much good with your life if you just applied yourself.

And to think I would never hear those words again.

I wasn't a son; I was a problem to be solved. It wasn't enough that I had gone to law school *for him*, spent three extra years of my life in a classroom listening to law professors teach about ethics and debate the Constitution... All of it was bullshit.

Such bullshit... because it didn't matter now.

The walls feel as though they're closing in on me and my chest begins to feel heavy, making it hard to breathe.

Why couldn't he understand that I wasn't him, that I didn't *want* to be him?

How could I ever compete with the great Kerry Walker? I wasn't meant to walk in his footsteps. His feet are – *were*, shit, *were* – too large, and his shadow too long for anyone to notice me, unless I was arrested for public drunkenness or a bar fight, which I realize is a very real possibility at this moment.

All I can think about is that I would never get another lecture from my father while he sat behind his large desk, looking at me with disappointment, and the words of that Emerson poem that he loved so *fucking* much comes tumbling out of me with much less grace than Emerson deserves.

The word of the lord by night,
to the watching pilgrims came,
as they sat by the seaside,
and filled their hearts with flame.

When I open my eyes and look around the bar, shocked faces, and some with amusement, look back at me and I realize I'm standing on top of a table, spilled beer clinging to my shoes. Before security can pull me down, I finish the poem, because when I commit to doing something, even if it's something stupid, I'm all in. At this moment, the final line of the poem feels especially appropriate.

God said, I am tired of kings,
I suffer them no more.

The crowd fills the space with loud cheering, but it could be my performance or the fact that I'm being dethroned from my perch on the table and effectively silenced.

"Get your hands off me!" I yell as I'm dragged towards the exit by Tony the bartender.

As if I have the need to make this situation even worse, I take a swing at him, but I miss due to my inebriated state and my impaired depth perception. I feel the blow knocking my head back but there's no pain, just the darkness that swims at the corner of my eyes. I blink a few times until I'm able to focus again, seeing Tony looking at me with both pity and anger.

"Don't come back," he says in a gruff tone as I'm deposited on my ass outside of the bar.

I'm vaguely aware of people walking past taking no notice of me, as if I'm just one of the many homeless in the alleys of Vegas.

Swiping a hand through my hair, I push a few rogue pieces off my forehead. This isn't the first time I've been thrown out of a bar, but tonight – tonight everything feels different – feels more – like an exposed nerve ending being irritated, and it pulses through me like a live wire.

Placing a hand to the ground I try to prop myself up, but the whiskey swirling around inside of me makes that impossible, so I give in and lean against the wall. If I could fall asleep I would welcome the darkness, but I can't get the images of the mangled helicopter out of my mind. Thoughts of my mother's face swim against my eyelids. I open them to get rid of the image.

It takes a moment for my vision to regain focus, but in front of me are a pair of high heels attached to the sexiest fucking legs I've ever seen. My eyes roam unabashedly higher and higher to the hem of a black dress, and Jesus Christ, if I leaned forward just a smidge more, I think I might be able to see her panties.

"I've never heard anyone quote Emerson while they were drunk," she says, and her voice is sweet like honey and almost childlike – such a contradiction to the curves of her body and those goddamn perfect legs. "Hemingway, yes," she continues, cocking her head to the side, taking me in, "but Emerson?" She clicks her tongue. "No."

Her statement makes me laugh and I lean my head back against the wall, if only so that I can look at her face. Her pink-dusted cheeks complement her pale blue eyes, and her hair framing her face is the color of a wheat field from a Van Gogh painting, a portion of it held back by a red ribbon.

I can feel myself sobering up, and I don't like it because everything is becoming lucid, and I'd prefer it not be. Maybe this is a dream. Maybe I did fall asleep. It wouldn't be the first time I'd had a wet dream in the form of a gorgeous blonde with legs for days.

Just to prove that she's real, I run a finger up her calf, and yes, she's real because even in a dream, no woman's leg feels this soft. She doesn't flinch; instead, she just moves her leg out of reach as if I got caught touching the merchandise without paying first. Smiling, I sit up a little straighter, pressing my back to the wall to get leverage so I can push myself into a standing position. As soon as I do the alley spins, and I pinch my eyes shut for a moment to get my bearings until the blackness fades away.

"Hemingway was a waste of a human, but a brilliant writer," I state while managing to hold her gaze.

"And you think Emerson was a great human being with a subpar knack for prose?"

"I don't think *anything* of Emerson," I say angrily—because I really don't.

"Just enough to quote him while you're drunk, which is quite impressive," she adds.

"Do you have a thing for guys that quote Emerson while they're drunk? Because if you do, I have a whole catalogue up here," I pause and raise an eyebrow, tapping my head, "just waiting."

She shakes her head and looks as if she wants to laugh, but she doesn't. "I don't."

"Surely you have better places to be than arguing about literature with a drunk."

"I just—" she falters, as if she's trying to frame her words carefully, "wanted to make sure you were okay." She holds a bejeweled clutch under her arm and pulls the jacket closer around her shoulders. I don't feel the chilly air. I don't feel anything, but I can see goosebumps pebble against her skin. I would offer her my jacket, but it's covered in whatever the fuck is on the ground, so I don't bother.

"Hopefully Tony didn't hurt you," she adds, looking at my eye which has finally started to throb.

"I probably deserved it," I admit, shrugging.

"Probably? You were pretty obnoxious."

"I have no doubt. I just wish I had more time to do so. I could have quoted Hemingway for you," I tease, lifting a conspiratorial eyebrow.

"You're an obnoxious, charming sort of drunk, aren't you?"

"Well, I suppose if one had to be a drunk, a charming drunk is the best kind," I agree.

"I wouldn't agree that's something worthy of achieving," she says in a smart aleck tone that I find very sexy—even if it's meant to be an insult.

"You should call yourself a cab." Her voice is laced with concern but not pity, even though I probably deserve it.

I've just been thrown out of a bar and I should go home. I should call a cab, but then I remember… "I don't have a phone."

"You don't have a phone?" she laughs.

"I threw it in the garbage."

"Well, that was a stupid thing to do."

"I do a lot of stupid things," I say, which is the truth.

"I can see that." She chews on her lip as if she's working something out in that pretty little mind of hers. "Just get home safe," she says, and when she starts to walk away, the prospect of never seeing her again dawns on me. "How much?"

I realize my assumption is coming from a place of privilege and general assholery but I say it anyway, because the only thing better then drinking yourself into oblivion is *fucking* yourself into one.

She slowly turns around, piercing me with those pale blue eyes, and God, I can feel them burn right through me. My heart starts to speed up as if each beat has a name, pressing into me with such assured force. It could be the coke from earlier or the many, *many* glasses of whiskey I had tonight, but I don't think so.

"Excuse me?" She tilts her head, the wheat-colored locks falling over her one shoulder, and I want to reach out and feel the silky strands between my fingers in the same way I want to run my hand up her leg and under her dress. "You think I'm a prostitute?"

"Look at me." I motion to my dirty jeans, and what I now realize is a tear in my shirt. "I'm not a cop." I manage to give her a charming smile in hopes it gives me a better chance. She hesitates for a moment while assessing me. If she's looking for some redeeming feature, some nobility like my father, she's not going to find it.

"I'm drunk and harmless." I give her a lopsided smile. Only a true self-respecting degenerate son of a senator would know an escort when he sees one. A very good one at that. So no, she's not a prostitute, but she does fuck for money. I know that much for sure.

She closes the few feet between us, and I think she's going to kick me in the balls. I move to block her, but she just looks me up and down in a way that makes my stomach tighten.

"You don't look like you could afford me." She tucks the little sequined purse further under her arm as if challenging me to either prove her wrong or give her a reason to stay. The sad look in her eyes gives me the feeling she doesn't really want to be alone either.

I pull out my wallet and show her my black card, along with a wad of cash.

She lifts an eyebrow and then looks around the alley as if we're going to be jumped any minute. I think that she's going to tell me to fuck off, which I would deserve, but instead she asks, "Do you have a room?"

"Yes," I reply, "but I need to stop somewhere first."

3
Heart of Gold

Evangeline

The elevator doors open to a spacious penthouse suite overlooking the Vegas Strip. The view is beautiful, but the room is trashed. The couch is dismantled, there's a huge rip in the felt of the pool table, and half-empty glasses sit on almost every surface like apocalyptic markers of a once-roaring party. But now it looks sad.

We stopped at a corner liquor store on the way to his hotel, where he bought a bottle of whiskey which is now about a third of the way empty. Quite a feat, since his hotel wasn't that far away.

I set my purse down on the top of the bar. Walking over to the wall to ceiling windows, my heels click on the wood flooring loudly, waking up the quiet space. The only other sound is his breathing and the rustling of his coat as he shucks it off.

I'm aware of his eyes upon me, cool hazel, but they're nothing like Senator Langley's—predatory, and assuming that everything, including me, was his. No. He doesn't look at me like that, but I've seen this look before, and it causes a flutter to rise in my stomach like a tiny butterfly.

He steps closer, and I lean against the cool glass. His dark hair is ruffled, framing his youthful face like a halo. He's young, handsome, educated, but most of all—a playboy. A playboy with too much money, and who is far too pretty for his own good. I can see little pieces of his father in him, those complicated hazel eyes and dark wavy hair.

"What's your name?" he asks, the head of the whiskey bottle dangling precariously between his fingers.

I recognize pain when I see it and it's etched all over his face, even though he tries to hide it with a charming smile. The indents on either side of his lips make him look vulnerable, heartbreak hidden behind that smile. We are both heartbroken.

Perhaps that's why I came up here with him.

No matter the reason, I have a lot to lose by being here. I'm not allowed to take dates without going through the agency. There's a strict non-compete clause in my contract, and breaking it would be detrimental – yet I risked it out of morbid curiosity.

"You don't need to romance me. I'm a sure thing."

He laughs, giving me a crooked grin, his incisors a tad too long, making his smile look admirably wolfish. He really is a charming drunk.

"I just want to know your name," he says.

I swallow. He's not a senator or a client. He's just a rich kid with too much time and money on his hands who just lost both of his parents.

I'm about to say my real name when someone steps out from the shadowy hallway. His blonde hair is messy and he stares at us with sleepy eyes, and I can't help but notice he's only wearing his boxers, although he doesn't seem to care.

"Dare, where the fuck have you…" He pads across the room and finally notices me, and a wide smile spreads on his face. "Oh," he says, and Dare shakes his head as if to warn him off, like he'll say something he doesn't want me to know. "I didn't know you had a," he pauses, looking me over, staring at my breasts and working his way down—"friend," he finishes, and darts his eye back to Dare for confirmation.

"Alistair," he says darkly as he sets the whiskey bottle on the nearby pool table.

Alistair slides his eyes back to me and I cross one ankle over the other while leaning against the glass. "I've never seen you before."

"Holly," the name rolls off my tongue like second nature, no second thoughts this time.

"Hello, Holly." Alistair says my name with an exaggerated tone and a sleepy smile that no doubt makes other girls fall to their knees. He then grabs Dare and pulls him to the side. I turn around and look out the window, giving them privacy although I can still hear them.

"Jesus, how drunk are you?" Alistair asks.

I hear Dare laugh darkly. "Not nearly drunk enough."

"Rausch has been calling me non-*fucking*-stop," I hear Alistair say.

"Not now."

I turn to see him shake Alistair off.

"You need to…" Alistair starts to say something but gets cut off.

"I need to take a piss," Dare announces unceremoniously and leaves the room. Alistair turns toward me, a grin spreading on his face, still in his boxers unabashedly. Why would he be embarrassed? Alistair is a good-looking man, with blonde hair, brown eyes, and the physique of a young man who probably plays lacrosse or polo – or whatever rich boys play.

Instead of taking in the view of the Strip, he's taking in the view of me.

"Where the *fuck* did Darren find you?" Alistair asks and clicks his tongue as he moves closer to me.

"Where else? A bar." Technically, it was an alley.

He looks me up and down once more, his expression turning curious. "What has he told you?"

I narrow my eyes at him. "I don't kiss and tell."

Alistair laughs. "No, I don't suppose you would." He drops the tip of his finger on my shoulder, dragging it lazily down my arm.

"Darren and I have been friends for a long time," Alistair says, his finger now reaching my elbow.

I lean in, looking up at him through my lashes. "Are you going to tell me that you and your friend share?" I ask, pulling my lips into a smile.

When Alistair leans in to kiss me, I slap him. The sound reverberates against the window and through the suite. He touches his cheek in obvious shock, and I can see his once playful expression turn to anger.

"Jesus," he spits and then reaches for me, but from behind him, Darren grabs his arm.

His eyes are bloodshot, the bruise on his face an ugly shade of purple and blue. He can barely stand, but he holds Alistair's stare.

I don't know if Alistair was going to hit me back. What men do when they're angry is never predictable.

Darren lets go of his arm and Alistair has the sense to look ashamed. "Mine," he says while shaking his head.

"Sorry," Alistair says in a flippant tone.

Darren turned from a charming drunk to an angry one.

"Get out," Dare says, pointing towards the elevators.

"Come on," Alistair cajoles and then slides his eyes to meet mine momentarily, probably assessing whether I'm worth fighting over. "You're in a bad state right now after…"

"I said *get out*!" Dare yells over him, his voice echoing in the room.

"What the fuck?" Alistair asks, looking down at his bare feet and boxers. "I don't have any clothes on!"

"I said get the fuck out!" Darren yells, stalking towards him, and Alistair backs up towards the elevator, reluctantly hitting the button.

"What am I supposed to do?" Alistair steps into the car.

"Figure it out," Darren snarls as the elevator doors close with Alistair in it.

"You didn't have to do that…" I'd rather leave than start trouble between him and his friend.

"Stay," he stops me with a gentle hand on my elbow. "Please," he adds, and I concede, letting go of my purse while Darren presses a hand to my back, leading me in the direction of the bedrooms. He stumbles, knocking into the edge of the pool table, gathering up the bottle of whiskey on his way.

Darren takes another drink from the bottle, and I can see the relief wash over his face as it further clouds his eyes. No matter what they say, the real reason men drink is because they want to forget, they want to hide in the murky waters it provides, to dull whatever pain is inside, and I remind myself that this is why I don't leave.

I put my arm under his to help him down the hallway,

and he turns us into the first room which I assume is his. He slides out from my hold and flops on the bed like a ragdoll. Leaning forward, he props his elbows on his knees, resting his face in his hands as he lets out a long sigh; a sigh that sounds as if he's releasing the weight of the world from his body.

He mumbles something that sounds like, *I'm a mess*. I want to tell him that we're all a mess, but instead, I stand in front of him and place my hand in his hair, running my fingers through the dark brown waves. Slowly, he lifts his head to look at me, the twisted colors of browns and greens in his eyes now engulfed by the darkened room, but the undeniable grief remains. I lift my leg and prop my heel onto the bed next to him, the skirt of my dress creating a curtain of silk. He runs his hand up my calf as if in utter fascination, and watches it disappear under the hem.

His hair feels like a down pillow. He wraps his arms around my leg and buries his head against my inner thigh, the softness of his hair against my skin making me sigh. I can feel his lips, warm and moist as he nuzzles against my leg, the tip of his nose reaching my panties. His breath makes me shiver, and everything tightens.

He runs his hands along my hips, fumbling with my dress to push it out of the way. I help him by grabbing the hem and sliding it over my head and tossing it to the floor. His hands remain at my waist as I stand before him in only my panties and bra, both a delicate black lace. He lifts his head to look at me.

"Jesus, you are even more perfect than I imagined," he whispers, pulling me onto his lap.

"I'm glad you like," I say, cocking my head and letting my hair fall to the side as I help remove his shirt which is ripped and dirty. He's lean but with well-defined muscles that I run my hands over, feeling his smooth skin.

He kisses the space between my breasts. "Let's see if every part of you lives up to my imagination," he breathes, reaching behind me and having trouble with the clasp of my bra. I lean back and unclip it for him. He slowly pushes down the black lace straps and I pull my arms free, letting the material fall between our bodies, exposing my breasts to him. His eyes on me are that of a man who is admiring a priceless painting, and my nipples pull hard and taut at the scrutiny.

"Worth every fucking penny," he groans, running a thumb tentatively over the nub and smiling when my body involuntarily shivers, the skin around my nipple pulling tight. His hands are gentle yet clumsy, moving over my body with wonder as he cups and pulls at my breasts, watching, almost mesmerized, by the way my body reacts to him.

I push the hair from his forehead, run my fingers through it, and grab onto a fistful, giving a tug. He groans against my breast and pulls me further into him, gripping my hips as I grind against him, but there is nothing to relieve the building ache.

He's not hard. I let out a disappointed sigh.

"Shit," he says with frustration, and releases my hips.

"It's okay," I whisper.

He leans his head against my chest, letting out a defeated breath.

"It's okay."

He pushes me off him and then falls back onto the bed, covering his eyes with his forearm as if to block out some nonexistent light. I sit on the edge of the bed next to him.

"It's not okay," he says. "Nothing is *fucking* okay."

"Darren…" I try to think of something to make him feel better. With the amount of whiskey he's consumed, I'd be surprised if he could perform.

He lifts his hips to pull the wallet from his pocket. "Just leave," he says. "Just take your fucking money," he yells and tosses his wallet on the bed next to me, cash spilling out.

"You don't have to pay me," I explain. "We didn't do anything."

"Jesus, do I have to be reminded?!"

"No, but I don't want to take money from you."

"A hooker with a heart of gold, how novel."

I glare at him. "Whatever cash you have is fine," I say, angrily.

"It's dangerous carrying that amount of cash in Vegas." He reminds me. "Besides, there's not enough."

"This is plenty." I try to grab the cash but he places his hand over it, piercing me with a challenging glare.

"I might be a fuckup and a shitty son," he says with deep regret, "but I always pay my debts."

Usually the agency takes care of payment, but this is different. I don't want to take money from him, but I hand him my phone anyway because of his persistence. If he knew why I was really here, it wouldn't end so amicably. "You can transfer it here." I tap on the account information.

Unexpectedly, he reaches over me to grab a laptop from the end of the bed.

"Don't have a phone, remember?"

I think maybe he'll be too drunk to execute the transaction, but then he hands my phone back to me and there's a large sum that's been deposited into my bank account. I feel sick, but I swallow it down.

Darren leans against the wall and covers his eyes with his forearm again, grabbing the whiskey bottle and slowly letting it pull him under its spell. At this rate, I'm afraid he might not wake up if he passes out.

I slide off the bed, kick off my heels, and pad into the living room, surveying the damage and wondering how Alistair is faring, only for a second, before making my way to the bar. The mini fridge is still full of tiny bottles of water, and I grab a couple, taking them back into the bedroom with me.

Darren is still on the bed, but now he's curled into the fetal position, the whiskey bottle tipped over next to him, his breathing even and soft. There wasn't enough left in it to make a mess, but there's still a small puddle seeping into the sheets. I take it from his limp hand and he makes only a small noise of protest as I set the two bottles of water next to the whiskey on the nightstand in the darkened room.

I contemplate leaving, like he told me to, like he wants me to, but when I look over at him, so vulnerable, alone, and looking so much like his father—I can't. So I slide back on the bed and lean against the headboard. It's one in the morning and I should be tired, but I'm not. I never got a chance to process the news that Senator Kerry Walker is dead. It doesn't seem real. I allow myself a few selfish memories that only bring me shame.

Darren rolls over and grabs onto my leg, inching his way up the bed until he drops his head into my lap. I'm not even sure he remembers who I am until he mumbles, "You're still here."

He's a grown man, but at this moment he looks more like a little boy, his head nestled on my lap, the softs waves of his hair dusting the tops of my thighs. I don't think I've ever felt young, and here, with him in my lap, I feel so much older.

I thread my fingers through his hair. "Yeah," I say and look down at him. "I didn't want something to happen to you," I explain, "you know, since you threw your friend out."

There's a moment of silence and I think he's fallen asleep, but then he whispers, "Fucking Alistair," in a sleepy voice, and I smile thinking of Alistair's face as he stood in the elevator as the door closed in nothing but his underwear. Maybe he didn't deserve being kicked out, but I can't help the mental image of him roaming through the casino in only his boxers.

Alistair seems like a clever guy though, so I'm sure he'll figure something out. It's quiet in here, so very quiet, and it's hard not to think of things I shouldn't.

"What's your name?" he asks out of the blue, suddenly lucid again.

I look down at him, my fingers stilling in his hair. "Holly," I tell him and close my eyes.

He's quiet for a minute. "Your *real* name."

I suck in a breath, thinking he probably won't remember in the morning before whispering, "Evangeline."

"That's a beautiful name." His voice is heavy with impending sleep.

After only a few moments, his mouth opens, and a little sigh escapes before he slips into a deep sleep. In the dark room, all I can hear is his even breathing that seems to mimic the ticking of the gold timepiece on his wrist.

On the bed next to me is his wallet, hundred-dollar bills spilling out, and I pick it up. Dare moves off my lap, curling onto his side and settling back to sleep, the whiskey pulling him under once again.

I sit on the edge of the bed holding his wallet and the money in my hand before grabbing my shoes and dress from the floor. I take Darren's wallet with me into the living room. Pulling out my phone from my clutch, I tap on my contacts and send a message to Cleo.

I'm fine. Be home soon.

4
The Kingmaker

Darren

I throw my arm over my eyes, trying to block out the sun. Rolling onto my side, I feel the nausea roll through me, so I reach over to grab the wastebasket next to the bed and empty the contents of my stomach into it.

"Fuck," I rasp, my voice hoarse, and my throat feeling like I've swallowed sand.

I would happily fall back asleep, but the events of last night start to come back to me in pieces. I sit up gingerly, giving my head time to catch up with my body. On the nightstand are two bottles of water near the almost empty bottle of whiskey. I grab for the waters like a man on a deserted island and down them both, way too quickly.

I remember I wasn't alone when I passed out last night.

Looking around the room, I don't see any signs that my guest is still here. I look for my wallet, remembering that I tossed it on the bed last night, but it's not there. I toss back the sheets—it's gone.

Fuck!

Angrily I smack the whiskey bottle off the table and watch as it careens across the room. What little contents that were left in it arc through the air and land on the carpet.

I sit on the edge of the bed with my head in my hands, trying to get up the nerve to face the day when I hear the shower running.

I lift my head and notice the crack in the slightly opened door, steam drifting out and causing the room to feel thick and humid. My body instinctively leans to the side to allow a view all the way into the bathroom.

Through the frosty glass doors of the shower, I can make out the outline of a woman's body—from the swell of her breasts to her small waist, the curve of her hips, and finally the generous roundness of her ass. Even though I'm sitting here with a horrendous hangover, I still want to sink my teeth into it.

Rising from the bed, I slowly make my way towards the bathroom, my bare feet making no sound on the carpet. I stand in the doorway and push it open wider as she pushes the water through her hair, her head tipped back, eyes closed, causing my pulse to quicken.

She didn't leave with my wallet.

She didn't leave, period.

She tilts her head and makes eye contact with me. The beautiful blues burn into me, beckon to me, and *fuck*, I've already paid for her. I step further into the room, the steam thick and heavy, while she watches me, the curve of her lip tempting and taunting me. Now that I'm fully sober and I'm no longer looking through whiskey laden eyes, I can tell she's worth even more than what I paid for her.

Water drips from her long eyelashes down her face and

pebbles at her perky breasts. The pale pink around her nipples puckers, and as my eyes lower further, I find that, *Jesus Christ*, she's fucking bare – so bare that I can see the soft, wet outer folds of her cunt.

I swallow hard.

Unlike last night, I have no problem getting hard.

In fact, my cock twitches and presses painfully against my jeans. Just the sight of her in the shower, her perfect body, causes my stomach to tighten as if there's a cord pulling me from the inside – pulling me towards *her* – and I find myself stepping into the shower fully clothed. Tipping my head back I open my mouth, letting the water fill it before letting it overflow, washing away the staleness.

All I can do is stare at her, paralyzed, overcome by how much I want her. She lifts her hand to touch the bruise at my eye and I wince. My whole body feels bruised, and every muscle protests any movement. I miss the alcohol numbing the pain, but having her naked and in my shower is better than any glass of whiskey, even the most expensive Macallan. I can almost guarantee that her cunt will taste just as sweet too.

Besides, I want to feel this. I want to remember every fucking detail.

The hot water feels so good, washing away the dirt and sins from last night—it would take more than just one shower to wash away all my demons.

She runs her fingers over my chest and down to my abs, undoing the button and pulling down my zipper. I step out of my wet jeans—heavy and awkward – and kick them to the side while she grabs the sponge and runs it over my shoulder and across my chest, leaving soapy bubbles in their wake. I let her clean me because it feels good, and I like watching her. Purposefully she positions her body flush to mine so I feel her erect nipples slide along my soapy chest. My balls pull tight, and fuck, it is taking everything in me not to slam her against the shower wall right now.

Instead, I drop to my knees like I'm praying at an altar, because I've wanted to taste her pussy since the moment I met her. I'm practically salivating for it. Her bare cunt is at my eye level, and I'm mesmerized at how the water flows over her mound and magically disappears into her slit. I run my thumbs along her outer folds before I spread her open revealing her world to me, and the excitement is heightened by the feel of her hands in my hair, pulling at the strands while I slip my tongue inside to taste her.

I'm a horrible person—a horrible son—for wanting this so much, for taking pleasure in the sight of this woman's bare cunt, in light of everything that happened last night – in light of everything I'm running from, but this is too good, and her low, sweet moans take me to a place even the bump of coke didn't last night.

If I have to run, I will run to booze and pussy every time – it's my character flaw, but as I draw my finger up her length to expose the nub of her clit and feel it pulse like a living, breathing thing – I will take this character flaw over any other.

I look up her body from my position kneeling before her, and watch as her eyes flutter closed and the water falls over her plump lips while I bring her close to climax. I'm mesmerized, so fucking gone as I watch beads of water fall over her skin onto her breasts and down her stomach where I collect them with my tongue like a starving man as I kiss and lick her pussy.

I'm driven by basic biology, the release that only

fucking can resolve. Her sweet moans are muffled by the pounding water as I eat her, gripping her hips while she rocks into me, harder and faster until her palms hit the glass with a force that threatens to break it. Her pussy grips my fingers, pulsing around me while she cries out.

Reaching outside the shower I grapple for my jeans, trying to find the pocket and pull out a condom. I can't seem to get it open fast enough. My balls are aching, and my cock is throbbing against my stomach. I want to fuck her against the shower wall, to thrust into her until the water runs cold and she begs me to stop.

We haven't spoken, not a single word since I stepped into the shower, and yet, she understands what I need.

I need *her*.

That's exactly what she gives me.

I hold her up as she wraps her legs around me, her chest flush to mine, nipples hard and rubbing against my skin. The friction and feel of her runs through my veins and straight to my cock. The minute I sink into her I can't stop, and nothing satisfies the ache inside of me. I want more and more until her breaths are nothing but short gasps and my muscles ache from the strain. She feels too good, and I am too far gone to be gentle. I don't feel it until the last minute, too late to stop myself from coming apart, and as I do, every emotion in my body starts to unravel like a ball of twine falling off a table. My body shudders against hers and I sink my face into the side of her neck, resting it there as I feel everything let go, my cum, my anger, and mostly, my grief.

The water is now lukewarm but it still hides the hot tears that spring from my eyes because I'm suddenly struck with the notion that I'm alone. The only person I have is a fucking prostitute I paid to fuck me so I can forget that my parents are dead.

The shower stall becomes too quiet, and I'm all too aware of my own breathing. I set her down gently, slowly unfolding myself from her, but I'm still not able to look her in the eyes as I step out of the shower, not bothering to grab a towel or worry about water dripping all over the floor.

As an afterthought, I slip off the condom, depositing it into the trash. From behind me I hear the shower turn off as I shake the water from my hair, continuing out of the bathroom. I push the hair from my forehead and stop dead when I see Rausch with his arms crossed over his chest standing in the living room.

If anyone has the power to make my cock limp, it's Rausch.

I'm surprised to see a few wrinkles in his normally perfectly pressed dress shirt. To my right, his security man stands in front of the door, blocking my exit – not that I would while still being naked. I notice Alistair stand from his perch on the couch, still in his boxers, a solemn look on his face as if he's a child waiting out his punishment.

"Your parents are dead, and you trash a hotel room." His blue eyes look past me as he adds on, "And apparently fuck hookers."

I follow his gaze to see Evangeline coming from the bedroom, her hair still wet and dripping onto her shoulders while she holds her shoes.

"What makes you think I'm a hooker?" she asks as she slips on her heels.

Rausch assesses her carefully, his mouth pressed firmly in a tight line. "An educated guess."

"Don't talk to her like that, Rausch," I tell him angrily after seeing her shocked expression.

"Touching," he says in an annoyed tone, turning his gaze back to me.

I give Evangeline an apologetic look.

"Jesus Christ, Darren. Do you know how much this will cost to fix?" Rausch gestures dramatically to the trashed room. I notice the TV mounted on the wall is cracked, and I just now remember that I hit it on my way out of the room last night, looking down at my knuckles to notice the bruises only just now.

"Just have the hotel send me the bill."

"Money is not going to fix this," Rausch yells, "especially when you don't have any."

"You're not making any sense."

Alistair straightens. "Can we just calm down?"

"I don't think either of you fuckups really understand the gravity of the situation," Rausch spits, pinching his eyebrows as if he's talking to two disorderly students instead of two grown men. "Your parents are dead, and not only is that a difficult situation for Congress, but it also means your money – your *parent's* money," he makes a point to say, "is tied up in probate."

"Can you – just stop saying that?" I throw my hands up.

"That your parents are dead? No, because the sooner you wake up and join reality, the better."

"What do you mean, there's no money?"

"The money is locked up in probate."

I look up from the floor to meet Rausch's satisfied gaze, and in a matter of a second, I upturn the coffee table, the contents scattering across the room. The security man makes his way over, but stops when Rausch raises his hand.

"What the fuck do you mean, probate?" I question, staring at Rausch with my chest heaving.

"You went to law school; did they not teach you about probate law?" Rausch doesn't rattle easily, that's why he got the reputation he has. Unbreakable, formidable, and effective – *The Kingmaker*.

Of course I know about probate law, and that means my parents money could be frozen anywhere from six months to two years.

I'm mad at Rausch for being the only one I have right now. I'm mad at myself for being such a fuckup. I'm mad at the pilot for crashing the helicopter. I'm mad that I feel *anything*.

"Is that what you think I'm worried about?" I ask him.

"You have worried about no one else but yourself, *Darren*, your whole life," Rausch lectures. "What do you think your mother would say if she saw you right now?" His eyes travel south, and then over to Evangeline, who is still standing next to me, eyeing the exit that is still blocked by the security guard.

If I want to drink and fuck myself into oblivion, that's my choice, but it's a low blow to use my mother to get a reaction out of me. As much as I want to think that I'm invincible, there is a chink in my armor—my mother—and Rausch knows it.

"Jesus, Dare." Alistair hands me a pair of shorts, even though it's too late for modesty and any sort of decorum.

"This is what I'm talking about." Rausch points to the overturned table. "It's exactly why your parents put stipulations in their wills."

I pull on the shorts and toss my hair out of my eyes. "Stipulations?" I ask, cautiously.

"Yes, Darren. If you weren't being such a fucking child, you would listen to me," Rausch continues, and he's right. I don't want to listen to him, but he has me in a stranglehold right now, like a boa constrictor around my neck. Worse yet, he knows it.

My father rarely discussed business with me, and he certainly didn't make me privy to his will or his wishes, should something happen to him. He certainly wasn't anticipating dying in a helicopter crash with my mom and leaving me alone to figure things out.

When I look at Rausch I take that back, because my father did anticipate such things, he just put Rausch in charge—not me. He never would have trusted me to handle his estate. Right now, I'm at Rausch's mercy, so I keep my mouth shut while the anger burns through me.

"You don't get any money until you're thirty years old," Rausch says, and then after a dramatic pause, adds, "or married."

Jesus fuck!

He'll make me beg, give me condescending lectures, and torture me for the next three fucking years. My heart sinks into my stomach, and Rausch can see it all on my face – the realization that he owns me. A satisfied smirk appears on his mouth.

Perhaps if I had been the good son, stayed out of trouble, listened to him more, prayed at the altar of Emerson, who he loved so fucking much, maybe then he wouldn't have put Rausch in charge of his affairs.

I narrow my eyes at Rausch because I've never been known to back down from a fight, and I still have skin in this game. It's an impulsive move, but dire situations require dire action. I grab Evangeline, pulling her to my side. "Well, isn't it convenient that my fiancée is right here?"

She looks at me with shock on her face. I lean in with a pleading look to kiss the side of her neck and whisper, "*I'll pay you extra.*" Whether that has any weight with her or not after what she just heard, I don't know, but I slip my arm around her waist and tug her closer.

"Are you fucking serious?" Rausch laughs.

"Very." I narrow my eyes at him in challenge, because I am done fucking around.

"You wouldn't dare." His demeanor changes as he realizes that I am *very* serious, because I have a lot to lose.

I fix my gaze on Rausch, glaring back at him. "Try me."

Alistair makes a strangled noise behind me that I ignore.

"Isn't it convenient that we're in Las Vegas," I taunt him. "We could get married today, right baby?" I dig my fingers into her side, and she returns the favor by digging her heel into the top of my bare foot.

Fuck!

Rausch's eyes narrow. "This is beneath you, Darren. All these years I thought *he's gonna wake up one day, figure his shit out*. Especially now, with your parents gone." I can see the deep lines in his brow, his grief hidden somewhere behind his anger towards me.

"This is me figuring my shit out." I gesture toward Evangeline.

Rausch runs a hand over his jaw and down his chin, looking between Evangeline and me.

"I would say that the two of you deserve each other, but then I'd feel sorry for her." His eyes roam over Evangeline.

I feel her straighten next to me. "You don't have to feel sorry for me," she speaks up. "Darren here is a great lay, and from what I gather, he's loaded – or at least he's gonna be. What's not to like?"

The look on Rausch's face makes me want to die with laughter, and I have to press a fist to my mouth in order to contain it.

"I'm not *fucking* around anymore, Darren. I want *you* at the airport in an hour! And I want *you* to go back to whatever street corner you came from."

"You shouldn't talk to the future mother of my children that way!" I call after him as the elevator doors close with him in it.

Evangeline shakes me loose, and I lift my foot to inspect it. "Jesus, is there a fucking hole?"

She stands with her arms crossed over her chest and a haughty expression gracing her face. "If there is one, you deserved it. What the fuck is wrong with you?"

I narrow my eyes at her, but then I hear Alistair's muffled laughter from behind me and I whirl around.

"I was going to say I'm sorry I threw you out last night, but…"

"I deserved it."

"Where did you sleep?" I ask sheepishly.

"On the bench outside the elevator banks, until Rausch found me," he explains. "Not something I recommend waking up to." He gives a half smile, and I imagine that to be true.

With Rausch gone, I feel like I can finally breathe.

"This is all very touching, but I should get going," Evangeline interrupts, heading towards the elevator.

"I propose, and you're leaving?" I ask, half teasing.

She turns to face me, and I can see her nipples through

the thin material of her dress. But that's not what threatens to get me hard again – it's that defiant little smirk of hers. "You must still be drunk," she says and then forcefully hits the button to the elevator.

"But you said I was a great fuck, and baby, that was with a hell of a hangover. Just imagine when I'm at my full potential." I wink and she rolls her eyes at me.

"Darren."

"Yes, dear?"

She scoffs. "Good luck with everything."

"Just let her leave. You heard what Rausch said," Alistair says from behind me.

"I heard exactly what he said." I grit my teeth and then turn back to Evangeline. I can't let her leave, she's my contingency plan. I will not let Rausch win, even if it means I have to play dirty. "And you're not going anywhere."

"You got what you paid for," she says. "Why would I stick around?"

"Because someone as exquisite as you would most certainly work for an agency," I explain. "Despite my reputation, paying for pussy isn't something I have a ton of experience with. Alistair, on the other hand, is more versed in the art of hiring escorts."

"I'm not sure that's a compliment," Alistair interjects.

"Any ideas which agency she's with?"

Alistair gives Evangeline a careful once over as if there's a price tag with the agency's name written on it.

"There's only a few reputable high-end places here in Vegas."

"Give me your phone," I demand and hold out my hand.

"What happened to yours?"

"It's probably on its way to a landfill by now."

"Here." He shakes his head and hands me the phone reluctantly.

Evangeline watches as I scroll through the phone. Finding the number I need, I hit dial and hold the phone to my ear.

"Hello," someone answers. "Yes, can you tell me if Ellen is available?" I watch as her eyes go wide, and the little pulse in her neck thrums like the beating of a hummingbird's wings.

"Oh, that's too bad because I personally wanted to thank her for sending over Holly—or is it Evangeline—I never know what the protocol is," I tell the woman on the line when she says Ellen is indisposed.

Evangeline makes her way across the suite to me. The expression on her face looks like she's ready to commit malice.

"We met in a bar last night, and she was worth *every* penny," I smile.

"What did you do?" she asks in horror, trying to grab the phone away from me, but it doesn't matter, the damage is already done.

"Consider it an insurance policy. I need a wife, and now you need the money."

"Is that why you insisted on transferring money to my account?" she accuses.

"Do you think I'm a fucking fortune teller?" I counter back angrily, seeing how her expression changes. "Is that why you wanted so badly to just take the cash, so there wouldn't be a trail?"

Her eyes narrow. "You're a prick!"

"Not the first time I've heard that."

"I knew I shouldn't have come here." She checks her

purse, presumably to make sure she hasn't left anything behind.

"Don't forget, you need me."

"We'll see about that!" she shouts, visibly shaking with anger. She turns on her heel and walks back to the elevator. I feel sorry for the button as she jabs it, but better the elevator than me.

Before the doors close, I say, "I need an answer tonight."

5
Pretty Girl Like You

Evangeline

As soon as I enter our apartment, Cleo jumps up from the couch, still wearing her sleep shorts and tank top. Her curly hair is pulled back by a headband. She looks like she's ready for a sleepover.

"Where have you been?" she asks in a worried tone.

I throw my keys on the counter, along with my clutch, and step out of my heels.

I met Cleo when I was a cocktail waitress, fresh off the heartache of losing my scholarship and having to drop out of college. At the time, I'd thought I was making good money with tips from high rollers, but Cleo was the one who told me I could make more money on one date than I made in a whole month's worth of tips. I remember so clearly the way she took me by the chin and said, *pretty girl like you shouldn't be working so hard in this dump.*

She introduced me to a life I didn't know about before, and now I just jeopardized everything because I'd let my guard down.

"What's wrong?" she asks when I don't answer.

"I messed up," I say, my voice small, and I work to keep my chin from quivering.

"What happened? Did someone hurt you?" She inspects me for damage, but there's nothing to find on the outside.

"I need to see Ellen," I say, walking into my bedroom and peeling my dress off.

"You don't just go *see* Ellen," Cleo reminds me as she follows me into the closet where I pull on a pair of jeans. "Unless something really big happened," she says ominously.

"Darren Walker happened, that's what," I begin to explain while I throw a shirt over my head.

"You mean the son of Senator Kerry Walker, the one that just died in that helicopter crash?" she asks in shock, pointing towards the living room where the news is playing on the TV.

"I already know I made a huge mistake, and he told Ellen about us in order to get me to marry him so he can get his inheritance." Saying those words just makes the anger grow hotter inside me.

"Excuse me, um, what century are we in?" Cleo asks, rearing her head back in confusion.

"It's a long story." I roll my eyes as I sit on the bed and pull on a pair of high heeled boots.

"I just can't believe you would jeopardize your contract —for what?" she asks angrily. "A fucked-up playboy who gets drunk and fucks escorts when he finds out his parents died?"

I wonder what she would say about me if Cleo knew the reason I went into that alley in the first place; because when he quoted Emerson on that table, it took me back to that place in my life when I needed some inspiration – and his father gave that to me.

"I don't expect you to understand."

"You're not really going to marry him, are you?" Cleo asks.

"I need the money." I take a minute to let it all sink in. "But I'm not just gonna lie down."

I grab my purse as I head into the kitchen.

"By the way, this came for you." Cleo motions to a box on the table.

Inside, I find a dozen red roses tied together with a ribbon. On the top is a handwritten card.

> *Hopefully we will get to finish our date soon.*
> *Xoxo,*
> *Jonathan*

Cleo lifts her eyebrows at me. "Who are they from?"

They're too big to fit, but I dump them in the garbage can anyway, leaving the long-stemmed roses hanging over the edge.

"No one important."

I'VE ONLY BEEN to Ellen's office once, and that was to sign my contract. Everything else has been done over the phone or in public somewhere to keep up the pretense that we were two unassuming people having coffee together.

I was just a young girl who never worried about how small my waist was or how large my breasts were, but I did know what beauty was, and how it could make you feel anything *but* beautiful. To me, growing up, beauty wasn't something I wanted to be known for. It made me visible, and that wasn't a good thing.

As soon as I open the glass doors, the woman behind the desk stands up.

"You're not supposed to be here."

"I need to speak with Ellen," I demand. "Tell her it's Evangeline Bowen." I use my real name because there's no hiding from the truth here.

"I know who you are, and Ellen isn't taking visitors," she says with an unfeeling voice, revealing that my suspicions are correct and I *have* been put on a list. A do-not-disturb list that I have no intention of adhering to.

Even so, my heart still beats rapidly at the thought of not being able to explain to Ellen what happened. There's a chance that if she'd just listen to me, I could get through to her.

"This is all a mistake," I explain, but I can tell by her stiff shoulders and pursed lips, she's not budging. "Please. I just need to talk to her," I resort to begging.

"I'm sorry, but…."

A feeling of helplessness takes hold of me and works its way up from my belly. I push past the receptionist, not letting her finish, and into the heart of the office. Only a few desks block my view of the office in the back where the privacy blinds are closed.

"Ellen!" I call out, my voice wavering like delicate fissures in a once sturdy wall. Another crack, and the wall might fall apart. I can hear the receptionist behind me, but I block out what she's saying.

"Stacia, it's fine," I hear Ellen's voice from behind me and whirl around. The receptionist retreats to the front of the office, and I'm met with Ellen's cool grey eyes. She's dressed far too lovely for such a bland space as this.

She walks past me with the expectation that I'll follow, which I do. Opening her office door, she sets her purse on top of the glass desk that looks so out of place with the rest of the office space.

"Take the money, Evangeline," she says coolly, taking off her jacket and hanging it on the hook by the door without looking at me.

"Ellen, it isn't what you think." The words tumble out of me like water skipping over rocks.

"Did you go back to his suite?" she asks.

"Yes, but he was drunk, and I couldn't just leave him in the alley..."

"Did you let him fuck you?" she interrupts.

I could lie and say that he couldn't get it up, but then how do I explain what happened in the shower the next morning?

"Yes," I say with an unsteady voice.

"Did you accept payment for the act?"

"I didn't want to, but he..."

"Did you take money from him?"

I can tell she already knows the answer. I didn't take the cash, and because of that, there's a money trail.

"He did this on purpose to get me fired so I would have no choice but to marry him!"

She holds up her hand to stop me, and that one authoritative finger causes me to snap my mouth shut.

"Do you know how I've run my business for so long without incident?" she asks.

I stand in the middle of her office, holding myself tightly for fear that all my insides will spill onto the floor like the tears threatening to spill over my eyelashes.

"Discretion," she says. "The reasons why don't interest me."

"I didn't ask for any of this."

"But you did—the minute you went back to his room."

"I... I shouldn't have, but..." I stammer, not sure what to say next. I've been beating myself up over that decision from the moment I made it. I crossed an invisible line, and I can't go back.

"So you know the rules, and you did it anyway."

"I'm sorry," I apologize, knowing it's not enough.

"Do not think that it doesn't pain me, Evangeline," Ellen says, her face softening just a bit, but if it gave me any comfort, it's lost the minute she finishes. "You made me a lot of money. A girl like you," she looks me up and down "has only a few more years left, so that's why I say, take the money he's offering you. You won't have another chance like that again."

I shouldn't be disappointed, because I know better. I'm a commodity to her, I always knew this.

"Does Darren know?" She looks up at me, and I shake my head as if I don't know what she's talking about. "Does he know that you knew his father?"

6
Less is More

Darren

"Was that really necessary?" Alistair chastises me.

"I'm not heartless. She'll get paid well for it." I set down the phone Alistair had to buy for me, because apparently my credit card doesn't work anymore.

"If you say so."

"Don't tell me you're growing a heart, Alistair. It's unbecoming," I tease, giving him a daring look.

"I would never." He uses the same voice as when he imitates his mother and mimes clutching a string of invisible pearls.

I stare out the window, noticing how dirty Vegas looks in the daylight. It's as if the sun sheds a spotlight on all the things that are wrong—wrong in my life, and wrong with what I'm doing.

I press on, the laptop in front of me open to the document my lawyer sent over an hour ago. He'd already expressed there was nothing I could do, and after a conversation where he pointed out that I wasn't a member of the Bar, and how I couldn't possibly know more than him, we hung up, and I started doing research.

"Dare?"

I know what he's going to say, because grief is written all over his face. Now that Rausch is gone, we can both let our guard down. I sometimes forget that my parents were just as much a part of his life as they were mine. Our lives had always been tangled up together like the branches of a cherry tree, each growing in different directions, but still stemming from the strong and firm trunk of our upbringing.

Before he can say anything else, I stop him. "I know." I know that he's sorry. I know that he feels the loss, too. I don't need him to say it, because saying it will make it too real. It will bring that grief forward, and there will be nothing I can do to push it back.

We've never been good at the serious stuff—probably because we've never had to be. Our friendship was built on the basis of alcohol and pussy. I get the feeling we might have to learn now, or we will fall apart. And I can't think about losing another person in my life right now. Not when there is so much at stake.

A Metallica song starts to play through the Bluetooth. "Turn it up!" I signal to Alistair, and he does. The music pounds through the speaker and it helps me to think—like it did when I would study in school, much to the chagrin of my fraternity brothers who couldn't understand how I could retain anything with such noise. They didn't understand that the heavy sound of Hammett's Les Paul drowned out all of the other noise—the constant chatter that never ceased in the fraternity house, or the pounding of a baseball against the drywall.

Metallica helped me concentrate—and that's what I need to do right now.

Alistair shakes his head at me.

I sit at the bar with a computer in front of me, searching through probate law like my life depends on it. I've been staring at the screen for so long the words begin to blend together, and I haven't even thought about having a drink, at least not until I've looked through every case I can find.

It reminds me of late nights sitting in my dorm, preparing for Professor Delaney's dreaded debates. He could pull a case out that could derail my whole argument. I didn't rattle easily—not then, and certainly not now—which is why I'm thinking about him, because there's a case somewhere I haven't found yet where I can get myself out of this mess—where I don't have to get married to get my money. I could leave Vegas on the private jet I flew in on and get my life back in order.

Except I'd be lying to myself if I thought it was that easy. Getting control of my parent's money was only the beginning, but it would get me out from under Rausch's oppressive thumb. Running a hand through my hair, I rest my chin against my palm, thinking. I was watching Alistair make a fool of himself last night without a care, misquoting Emerson, until it all came crashing down on me. All of the carefully laid bricks of foolish pride and incredible privilege just blown away, lying in rubble at my feet.

Emerson—I hated him and his poetic words that won't or can't leave my brain, and that leads me to think of her—Evangeline—the way she looked at me, and the anger surfaces again, but not at her or Rausch, but at myself.

I push the pad of paper off the bar, and if I could punch

and throw everything in this room into a pile of rubble, I would, but I'm painfully aware of why that won't solve anything. It won't make me a good person—a good son.

Instead, I pick up the phone and pull up my favorites. There were only a few I'd saved for quick access—Alistair was one, a friend-with-benefits was another, but at the end of the very short list, was just the word: *Home*. I hadn't lived with my parents since before I went to law school, and even then, I barely lived there—sleeping in my childhood bed like it was a hotel room.

I hit the green call button, and hearing it ring, thinking someone will pick up, and I'd hear the dulcet voice of my mother who was always happy to hear from me—maybe too eager at times, and that always left me feeling guilty. I end the call before it goes to the answering service, because the reality is she will never answer that line again, and yet, as I stare at my phone, I know that I will never bring myself to remove that number.

"Find anything?" Alistair asks, entering the room freshly showered, and I tuck the phone in my pocket.

His hair is still wet, dripping onto his shirt, and the smell of his heavy aftershave fills the room.

"Anyone ever tell you less is more?" I wave my hand in front of my nose to clear the fog of Cartier. "You smell like an eighth grader going on his first date."

"Gotta give it time to settle," he says, gesturing with his hand.

With a heavy sigh, I close the laptop. "I think I might have to admit defeat."

"Never thought I'd hear a Walker utter the word defeat."

"Don't worry, Alistair." I look at the time and grab my coat. "I'm not going home empty handed."

7

Bluebloods Run Cold

Darren

There was a small part of me that worried she wouldn't come – that little pebble of doubt that sat heavy in my stomach, but my offer was too good to pass up, and she knew it. I made sure of it.

As we sit across from each other at the diner – even though she doesn't hide her disgust with me – I know that she's made peace with her decision. I might be the biggest asshole in her life right now, but I had no other choice… at least that's what I tell myself.

"You're not the first man to propose marriage," she says, crossing her arms over her chest and pursing those oh so luscious lips, "although you are the first one to ask while not fucking me." She cocks an alluring eyebrow.

She says it to shock me or to bait me, and I'm all too willing to be baited, especially by her. I imagine the polite smile on her face, knowing that just the sight of her naked body would make a man drop to his knees before her. I know I did, and I would do it again and again.

The wind blows a few strands of wheat-colored hair from her shoulder as one of the waitresses walks by in a hurry. The dinner rush is in full swing, and every table is taken.

"If you prefer that I ask while in bed with you," I smirk, "consider it done." My voice is low and raspy from lack of sleep, and I lick my lips before taking a sip of the coffee in front of me.

She graces me with another beautifully defiant smile, and I can't help but remember those lips as beads of water clung to them—the feel of her tight ass in the palm of my hand. It makes me hard just thinking about it, and yes, I realize how this makes me look, but I don't care. That is how much I want her.

She's my salvation, because I cannot wait three years to inherit my parent's money. I cannot let Rausch have control over me and see his condescending expression every time I would have to *ask* him for money.

I grip my cup of coffee tighter and concentrate on Evangeline's face.

"Is everything a game to you?" She shakes her head, causing her hair to tumble over her shoulders. "Do you play with people's lives because it's fun?"

"That's not what this is."

"Then what do you want from me?" she asks with a raised voice, and it sounds foreign and strained, so unlike her usual soft, sweet tone.

"Are you hungry?" I ask, and she looks at me confused. "I'm fucking starving."

She lets out a long breath and I think that she's going to leave, tell me to fuck off, and she'd have every right to, so I say, "It's a proposal."

Her beautiful blue eyes narrow.

"A *professional* proposal," I clarify.

She lifts an eyebrow, and I get the attention of the waitress to order a stack of chocolate chip pancakes with whipped cream and syrup like I'm a five-year-old, but I don't care. The waitress looks to Evangeline, but she just shakes her head. "I'm not hungry."

"She'll have the same." I thrust the menus at the waitress, dismissing her, while Evangeline glares at me for ordering for her.

"You don't have to eat it," I tell her.

She crosses her forearms, propping them on the table, and scoffs.

"What?" I ask.

"You don't care if it goes to waste. You've clearly never had to go without a meal in your whole life. Do you even know how many homeless there are in Clark County?"

I don't think she gives a fuck about homeless people; she just wants to take a jab at me.

"The homeless are not my problem," I say plainly. "But if you don't eat your fucking pancakes, then they become *your* problem." I lean back into the hard plastic bench seat of the booth just as the waitress sets our plates in front of us.

"Can I get you more coffee?" she offers.

"Yes," we say in unison, and then look away from each other. I try to focus on my plate while she focuses on anything but.

I don't think I've eaten a stack of pancakes faster in my life.

I lick the syrup from my fork, and she watches as I place it back down on my empty plate while hers remains mostly untouched, the whipped cream melting against the once hot pancakes.

I reach into my jacket pocket, pulling out a piece of paper and sliding it across the table.

"What's this?" she asks, looking up from the table, and not bothering to examine it.

"It's a contract," I explain.

In a strained voice, I start, "You heard what Rausch said." I shouldn't care what she thinks of me or my motivations, but there's a little pebble in the pit of my stomach that wishes she wouldn't look at me with such disdain. "I need to either be thirty – or married," I finish dramatically. Which is the reason she's here – the reason I asked her to marry me in a not so romantic way – if you can even call it that.

"I don't turn thirty for another three years, and that *fuck*, Rausch, will have control over everything until then," I explain.

"Looks to me like you might need someone to report to."

I scoff, running a palm over my face.

"You met Rausch. He can be more of an asshole than that, if you're wondering."

"Don't you have some debutante named Buffy willing to marry you?" she asks, taking a sip of her coffee. Her eyes are like blue flames peering over the cup at me, waiting for a response. She looks like she might kick me under the table at any moment, so I keep my legs from spreading out too far and giving her a target.

"That's not what I want." I level my eyes on her. "Bluebloods run cold, and from the taste I got, you're a red-blooded all-American."

She shakes her head in disgust. "I don't even like you."

"Even better. I don't need a romantic entanglement," I tell her. "Love has a way of complicating things, don't you think?" I notice when she swallows hard. "You're a professional, are you not?" I clarify, grabbing a toothpick from the container at the end of the table and rolling it around on my tongue.

She crosses her arms over her chest and leans back as if she's ready to listen.

"This is the contract." I drop my eyes to the paper in front of her. "One million dollars to be my wife."

She stares at me in disbelief.

Looking down at the contract, she pulls it towards her, and I watch as her eyes scan the document. I wish I knew what she was thinking, and wondering if she knows that I need this more than I need to breathe. I was serious when I said I don't need romantic entanglements. This arrangement is a means to an end, to get my money, and move on with my life.

"A year?"

"For it to be legitimate, yes."

"And I have to live with you?" she questions, looking up from the contract.

"You say that like it's a bad thing. I assure you, my home in Georgetown is more than satisfactory."

"Is it big enough where I wouldn't have to run in to you the whole year?"

I know she's trying to get under my skin, to let me know how much of an asshole I am, but if it means she'll sign the contract, I will swallow every insult she can throw at me. "Probably not." My eyes settle on her perfect pink lips and I wonder if they feel as soft as they look, and right now, I would do anything to find that out. "I'm not into fucking women against their will," I state with distaste, "if that's what you're asking. But if you *are* willing," I pause and cock an eyebrow, "you might even like it."

A contemplative look crosses her pretty face, and the part in her lips tells me everything I need to know—everything I felt in the shower. We want the same things.

"You politicians are all the same; making a jalopy sound like a Mercedes."

"I'm not a politician," I scowl.

"If you say so."

"You fuck men for money," I say crassly, but she doesn't blanch. "Would this be any different?" I ask.

Her lips tug at the corners, the start of a smile that never quite reaches her eyes, but I'll take it. I'll take it because it means she's giving in, she'll say yes… she has to.

"You can have someone look at the contract before you sign if you like, but it's a win-win situation for both of us."

She stops me, pushing the contract back across the table, and my heart stops beating as I hold my breath.

Her eyes snap up to mine, the blue turning dark and angry.

"You made it almost impossible for me to say no," she spits, but I can't help focusing on the 'almost' part, which causes a nervous flutter to beat inside my chest.

"It's the lawyer in me."

"The asshole part, or the contingency part?"

If I could, I'd bend her over this table right now and show her exactly how much she *would* enjoy being my wife. Her bratty behavior is threatening to make me hard. I have to make a fist under the table to tamp down the need.

"Both," I shrug.

"Five million," she says, staring back at me with hard, bitter blue eyes.

We stare at each other like we're playing a game of who can blink first.

"That's a hefty increase."

"Do you know how much money I make in one night?" she asks, running her tongue along her bottom lip. "That, times three hundred sixty-five days, and five million doesn't even begin to cover it."

"Are you offering up three-hundred sixty-five nights?" I ask, resting my forearm on the back of the bench seat.

"Did you know that most men hire an escort *not* to have sex, but for companionship? Someone to listen to them, a shoulder, or a lap to cry on?" she asks.

"Are you saying you're a therapist?"

"You seem like you could use one, but no."

Her witty comments make me laugh. I don't think I've ever met a more challenging woman then Evangeline Bowen.

"Five million or no deal." She has the stare of a great poker player.

I chew on the inside of my cheek for a moment as we stare at each other, the sparks threatening to burn up the table between us.

Relenting, I take a breath. "And I'm sure you'll be worth every penny," I groan while rubbing my chin.

I look down at her untouched plate of food.

"Aren't you going to eat?" I challenge, rubbing my chin. "All those poor hungry, homeless people."

A slow smile spreads on her lovely face as she dips her finger into the whipped cream, scoops up a large dollop, and brings it to her lips. Her tongue darts out in an alluring way, licking a small bit of the whipped cream on the end before sucking her whole finger into her mouth without breaking eye contact. So help me God, my cock jumps in my pants, and a groan escapes my lips.

I pull a pen from the pocket of my jacket, scratch out

the amount on the contract and write in the new figure. "I'll have my lawyer make it official later."

"Just one more thing," she says and it gives me pause, my heart leaping into my throat. "You didn't get down on one knee and ask me."

I settle back in my seat. "Ask you what?"

"To marry you, of course," she laughs, and then leans forward. "When you ask a woman to marry you, you're supposed to do it properly by getting down on one knee." She narrows her eyes. "Are you going to deny me something every girl dreams of?"

"Are you serious?"

"Dead." She crosses her arms.

"But I don't have a ring," I protest.

"Pretend." The dominant way she says it makes me pull at the collar of my shirt.

I slide out of the booth and awkwardly get down on one knee in front of her, the familiar position causing licks of heat to coarse over my skin. Kneeling in front of Evangeline, that sweet look on her face, and the way she blinks at me expectantly, I wonder how any man could deny her anything.

Slowly, the noise in the diner starts to dissipate, and when I look around, everyone is staring at us.

I clear my throat. "Evangeline Bowen, will you do me the honor of being my wife?" I ask and then lower my voice so only she can hear. "For five million *fucking* dollars," I grit out.

There's clatter all around us but I don't pay any attention to any of it. I just stare at her, waiting—and she takes her sweet fucking time.

"Yes, Darren Walker, I will marry you," she says in an overly sweet voice.

The diner erupts into applause, and I look around sheepishly. They start to chant *kiss her, kiss her, kiss her*.

I'm more than happy to oblige. I've been thinking about kissing her this whole time as I watched her bite, lick, and part those pretty pink lips during our negotiation. I pull her from the booth and press her body flush to mine. She swallows hard, and a small sigh escapes her lips. With my arm wrapped around her waist, I bring my other hand to rest against her cheek, brushing my thumb along her jaw. She looks up at me, blinking slowly. "Is this what you wanted?" I ask quietly.

"Almost," she smiles, and then presses her lips to mine. The chatter in the diner fades to background noise. When I slip past her lips with an eager tongue, I can already tell it's not nearly enough, especially when she tastes so sweet and her hand rests on my shoulder. Such a chaste move, but it makes me greedy for something that cannot happen in the middle of the diner. For a moment after she pulls away, I can see her searching my eyes, but I don't know if she finds what she's looking for.

The noise of the diner snaps back into place the moment her forehead leaves mine and she turns to face the crowd of curious patrons, her game face on once again.

"This man right here just won a lot of money, and he's too shy to say it, but everyone's meal is on him."

Another round of applause ensues and I narrow my eyes at Evangeline, very aware that my mouth is hanging open. "I don't have the fucking money yet," I grit out and watch as she gives me a satisfied smile.

"I'm sure you can figure something out. You're resourceful." She claps my shoulder with a wink.

As I look at her – young, pretty, and dangerous – I let out a long sigh. "Did you know the downfall of every powerful man is underestimating a beautiful woman?" I ask.

She leans down and signs the contract with a ceremonial flick of her wrist and sets the pen on top of it.

"You're not a powerful man, Darren Walker," she says, taking a bite of her pancakes. "Not yet."

"Grab your best dress, Evangeline," I order and hold out my hand for her, "Elvis is waiting."

8

Dainty Waist for a Man

Evangeline

"You aren't seriously doing this?" Cleo asks as she follows me into my bedroom where I grab my suitcase from the closet and throw it on the bed.

"I have no choice." I wasn't going to let Darren *fucking* Walker know that, though.

"You marry this guy, get your money, and then what?"

"Take my choice back," I say, turning towards her.

Cleo gives me an understanding smile. She places a hand on my thigh. "Money means different things to different people. You," she uses her finger to dig lightly into my thigh, "never struck me as someone who put that much importance on it."

Cleo is probably the only person who truly knows me, and even she doesn't know everything.

I laugh because she's right. Yet here I am, taking five million dollars to marry a man I don't know. I didn't need that much. One million would have been fine, but I wanted to make him pay for what he did.

"This guy could be a sadist or a psychopath."

I think back to the alley where all I saw was a vulnerable man at one of the lowest points in his life, in the shower, the way he placed his face against my neck, holding onto me as if I were a buoy in a rolling ocean. It doesn't make him a good person, in fact he's deplorable under the circumstances, but he's not a psychopath.

"He's an over-privileged rich kid who needs a wife to get his inheritance," I say absently, having already explained the terms to Cleo. She didn't like it, still doesn't, but I think she's more upset I'm leaving. We'd been living together for a couple years now, and had gotten used to being in each other's space. With her absence I won't have *my* anchor, and maybe she's worried about the same thing.

"I still can't believe everything that's happened. Darren Walker? I didn't even know who he was until his parents were all over the news," Cleo admits as she sifts through my clothes, trying her best to fold them while I make my way into the bathroom, grabbing some necessities. "I don't follow politics," she adds.

I can't help but laugh. Most of our clients are politicians.

Darren Walker might not be a politician, but he's a politician's son. Whether his parents are gone is irrelevant, because he'll always be inextricably entwined in a world of war games, and here I am, walking willingly into the fray.

"I can pay for my half of the apartment for the rest of the year," I offer as I walk back into the bedroom.

She waves me away. "I'm not worried about the money, I'm just worried about you."

I place the little bag of necessities into my suitcase, tucking it in much longer than needed, smiling at how Cleo has folded my clothing neatly. "I can take care of myself," I sigh.

Cleo grabs my hand. "I know you can, honey. I just wish, for once, you didn't have to."

What she says hits harder than I expected, and tears well in my eyes. I stay bent over the suitcase, pretending to organize my clothes until the tears go away. I close the top and zip it up before swinging it off the bed. It's very apparent that I don't have a lot. Cleo was right, money never meant much to me. All of the expensive items I have I received from clients. I've left them for Cleo – the coveted Birkin bag I never used, the diamond tennis bracelet I never wore, and a pair of shoes that cost more than my rent.

I didn't grow up with those things, and I knew better than to get used to them. This kind of life is hand to mouth, and it could all be gone tomorrow – case in point.

I wheel my bag into the living room and stand next to it. "What are you going to do?"

"Oh, you know me," she smiles, "I'll figure something out." She shrugs, causing her fluffy brown hair to bounce which makes me giggle – especially because she's wearing a pair of unicorn pajamas.

I reach out and run a hand along her arm. I've never been an especially emotional person, and I'm definitely not a hugger, but at this moment, I have an overwhelming need to hold on for as long as I can.

When I step off the elevator to the downstairs lobby, at the curb waits a black SUV, the windows tinted so dark I can't see inside, but I know it's for me. No one in this building would be picked up by this kind of vehicle unless it was decorated with strobe lights, penises, and the words '*Fling Before the Ring*' written on the back window. A man dressed in a black suit exits the driver's side and opens the back door for me.

I can see his strong jaw and pressed lips from the side. Even though he doesn't look at me, I begin to realize that he looks familiar.

I know him.

I'm sure of it, but even though I stop to look at him before getting in, his eyes never give away that he knows me too.

"Congratulations, Mrs. Walker," he says with a professional smile, and I think maybe he doesn't remember me as he takes the handle of my luggage and wheels it to the back of the SUV while I look after him curiously.

I'm about to correct him when I look inside the vehicle and notice Darren sitting in the backseat with a drink in hand, wearing a very nice suit. The white collared shirt is unbuttoned carelessly, and his black suit jacket is open, revealing a trim waist with the shirt tucked in nicely. I had only seen him in dirty jeans and wrinkled shirts, aside from the casual clothes he had on earlier at the diner.

But a suit looks—well, it looks *good* on him. I take a deep breath.

"What are you wearing?" he asks as I settle into my seat, and the driver closes the door behind me.

"What's wrong with what I'm wearing?" I ask in an annoyed tone, looking down at my jeans and sneakers.

The car begins to move, and I watch in the reflection of the window as my apartment shifts out of view.

"You can't wear jeans to get married," he scoffs, taking a sip of his drink.

"Does it matter?"

Darren just smiles, tossing the remaining finger of whiskey back, and then sets the glass on the bar next to him. "Of course it does." He turns his attention to the driver.

"Bailey, we need to make a stop first." He punches something in his phone that I presume are directions.

The SUV takes a turn and heads in the direction of the lights, like a moth to a flame. The traffic converges on the strip, and everything slows to a crawl. My eyes focus on the window, and in the reflection, I can see Darren staring at me, his hand rubbing at his jaw, but then the car moves again, and the image is replaced with lights from a nearby billboard.

Bailey pulls the SUV down a side street towards one of the hotels and stops at a portico. He gets out swiftly and pulls my door open before I can do it myself. Darren nudges me, and I step out onto the sidewalk, not really sure where we are or why. In a gentlemanly gesture, he holds out his arm for me to take, and I stare at him until he grabs my arm and pulls me with him.

I look over my shoulder to see Bailey pull the car away. We walk past all of the poker tables, the chirping slot machines, and into the heart of the casino, where the lights are dimmed and Roman statues line the walkway. When I look up, a fresco takes up the entirety of the ceiling. I've been here before with Cleo, window shopping, but their expensive price tags are beyond my means.

Along the walkway are designer shops with handbags and jewelry, art galleries, and expensive restaurants. Darren stops, and I almost careen into him. My stomach drops when I see what shop we're standing in front of.

"You can't be serious!" I exclaim, looking inside at all of the designer wedding gowns.

"We're getting married, Evangeline. You need a wedding dress, don't you?" His flippant tone annoys me.

"I'm not going in there," I grit and stomp my foot.

"You signed the contract," he says stiffly.

"Nothing in there says I have to wear a wedding dress." I cross my arms over my chest.

"You made me get down on one knee," he says through gritted teeth. "And I owe Alistair for buying everyone's breakfast, no thanks to you."

I can't help but laugh, but it's quickly replaced with a scowl.

"You find that funny?" he asks, a hint of a smile on his face as he looks at me.

"Nothing makes me happier than to see you uncomfortable."

"You don't have to resist every kind gesture I offer," Darren says.

"You think forcing me into marrying you is kind?" I ask, exasperated.

He rubs his chin. "Not when you put it that way. Look, most women would kill to wear a dress by this designer." He gestures to the shop window where fitted and full-skirted glittering wedding dresses are displayed, as if I'm supposed to swoon all over them.

"You like them so much, maybe you should wear one." I flick my hand at the dresses, realizing they must have a hefty price tag, and decide to make my way inside.

One of the saleswomen sees me walking through the aisle. I can tell she's judging me by the way she looks at my distressed jeans and sneakers with a wary eye. "Can I help you?" she greets, plastering a fake smile on her face.

"Yes, can I see your most expensive dress?" I stop in front of her.

She looks between me and Darren as if she's trying to figure out if we belong. Perhaps after recognizing Darren's expensive suit, or smelling his monied cologne, she relents.

"What size do you need?"

I look over at Darren, ignoring her snobbish attitude towards me. "You look like a fourteen to me."

"Excuse me?" Darren looks offended.

I reassess him. "You do have a dainty waist for a man. Maybe a twelve? What do you think?" I ask the saleswoman.

"Well, I'm—I'm not sure," she stutters.

"She's clearly joking," Darren tells her and then turns me away from the saleswomen. "I do not have a dainty waist," he whispers through gritted teeth.

I smile.

"I'll just give you two a minute," the saleswoman says.

"You're being difficult."

"Am I?" I stomp through the store flicking dresses out of my way.

He grabs a nearby dress and shoves it at me. "This looks like a nice dress." He holds up the strapless mermaid style dress to me as if he's judging whether it's my size or not.

"Not my style." I shove it out of the way.

Darren grabs another one, this time with a full skirt made of tulle, and I shake my head.

"You're going to make this a very long year," he huffs from behind me.

I don't expect Darren to understand—he's not a woman. Wearing a wedding dress is a big deal – not that I ever thought I would get married. I wasn't ashamed of who I am, but I'm not stupid enough to think that even if I did allow myself to fall in love, that man would fall in love with me, knowing what I am—what I've done. It's a double standard, but it's also reality.

Whenever I imagined getting married, because that's what little girls do, it wasn't to an infuriating, overprivileged child who played dirty to get what he wants. When I get to the end of the aisle, dresses falling on the floor in my wake, I stop short. Darren almost careens into the back of me, dresses in hand, as he tries to put them back on the racks.

"I bet my jeans and sneakers are looking really good about now?"

"You need to stop acting like a brat," he says, but I'm not paying attention to him.

In front of me is a dress made of delicate lace, the modest neckline and sleeves clinging to the mannequin in a way that looks both chaste and alluring. The material is not quite white, but aged or vintage, the way clouds can look sometimes right before rain.

Darren stands next to me, breathing heavily, as if he'd just had a workout. He's quiet for a moment.

"I think you would look exquisite in that dress," he says quietly. He looks at me without any pretense or condemnation, and for a moment, I see the man in the alley who was vulnerable and too drunk to hide it. There's an uncomfortable silence, and all I can hear is my own breathing as my heart thuds rapidly against my chest.

I turn away from the dress and find something gaudy and expensive looking.

"You want me to wear a wedding dress?" I ask, shoving the dress at him. "This is my size."

9
Elvis Tribute Package

Darren

"How many people can say they got married by Elvis?"

She points to the sign at the entrance. "Apparently, over eight hundred thousand."

Bailey opens the door on Evangeline's side and helps her out. The trail of white chiffon falls out of the car and onto the concrete like a waterfall.

"Let's get this over with," she sighs.

Evangeline picks up the skirt of her dress and marches across the parking lot, her ass swaying defiantly the whole time, and I am oh so helpless to follow her.

An elderly woman greets us at the small front desk area. "Walker wedding," I say, and Evangeline clears her throat while the woman looks at her computer.

"I have you down for the Elvis Tribute package."

Evangeline grabs my arm. "I thought you were joking," she grumbles.

"What's a Vegas wedding without Elvis?" I pull a sarcastic face and shrug.

"Oh, Harold's a wonderful Elvis, you'll love him. Looks just like him," she laughs.

"Harold," Evangeline whispers into my ear with amusement.

"Do you have anyone else in your wedding party?"

"It's just us." It comes out sounding sad without meaning it to, but Alistair already went back home earlier today, so it's just us.

"I'm Marla, and I can be your witness. You can wait over there until the chapel is ready." She motions to a seating area off to the side of the entrance.

I take Evangeline's hand and lead her to the bench. One of the many doors open and a couple walk through, along with their wedding party. Music and loud voices fill the small waiting area.

She watches the wedding party go by with a forlorn look on her face, and I almost feel guilty… almost.

Once they leave the space is filled with an awkward silence, and I fidget with my father's watch – the one he gave me when I graduated law school – while we wait. The action calms my nerves but also serves to be a reminder and I'm helpless against the emotion.

Evangeline looks down at my hands and I'm about to explain, but then Marla interrupts.

"They're ready for you now," Marla says, and ambles through the open door and into the chapel.

At the end of the aisle is a man dressed in a sequin jumpsuit, jet black hair coiffed perfectly, and large, bejeweled sunglasses covering his eyes. Evangeline's horrified expression is enough to make me laugh. Here she is in a designer wedding gown amidst this gaudy affair, and it's fucking perfect.

When *Love Me Tender* starts to play from the speakers in the corner of the chapel, I swear she gives a little snort.

"Ah, such a beautiful couple," Marla effuses, and clasps her hands in front of her. I'm sure she says this to all the couples who come through here.

"Now, I have to ask if both of you are willing participants," she asks bluntly.

"Define willing?" Evangeline asks, and I but my hip into hers.

"I just have to make sure neither of you are drunk," she clarifies.

Evangeline leans into me and says, "If she asks for a breathalyzer, you might be fucked."

"Would you like me to walk in a straight line?" I ask pointedly.

"That won't be necessary," she says sweetly. "If you'll give me the marriage license, I'll make sure it gets signed prior to you leaving."

I hand her the paper and fix my suit. Before the music fades, we walk up to our Elvis, who tells us to take each other's hands and repeat after him.

"You're not going to be a runaway bride, are you?" I tease.

She gives me a saccharine smile. "I have five million reasons not to, Darren."

The challenge in her blue eyes causes a groan to form in my throat and excitement to build in my stomach, pulling at my balls like the tightening of a string, and she holds the fucking end of it.

"Do you, hunka, hunka, Darren, take Evangeline, to be your lawfully wedded wife, until death do you part?"

"Or the contract is over," she says quietly through gritted teeth.

"Do you know what happens to brats?" I ask, and she tosses her hair back defiantly.

I narrow my eyes at her when I say, "I do."

"Do you, Evangeline, take hunka, hunka, Darren to be your lawfully wedded husband?"

She swallows hard but keeps her eyes trained on me. There's no doubt in my mind that she hates me. She has every reason to.

She's silent, and I swear I hear crickets in the room. She's taking her time, as if she's contemplating her answer. "I do," she finally says in a soft voice.

"Do you have the rings?" Elvis asks, looking at me expectantly.

"Shit," I say, dropping her hands, and Evangeline rolls her eyes at me.

"I have some you can purchase from the gift shop." Marla steps in.

"Does this happen often?"

"You'd be surprised."

I nod and she hurries out of the Chapel.

Evangeline shifts in her heels impatiently, and Elvis tries to reassure me that forgetting the rings isn't a sign of a doomed marriage. Giving him a menacing glare shuts him up until the woman returns a few moments later with two rings.

"Do people actually wear these?" I hold one in my hand, a pair of dice replacing what would be a diamond. Evangeline scoffs and shakes her head at me as if I'm the biggest moron on the planet. The other ring is adorned with dice etched into what feels like aluminum and holds the promise of making my finger turn green.

"Oh yes," Marla says eagerly. "It's one of our best sellers."

Evangeline smirks and I glare at her while I slip the ring on her finger. "I'll get you a nicer ring, I promise."

"Not necessary." She shoves the ring on my finger and it catches on my knuckle before sliding down, and I think it might cut off circulation.

"I now pronounce you husband and wife," Elvis says with a shake of his hips. "You can now kiss your bride."

Can't Help Falling in Love plays loudly through the speakers, and my eyes fall to her full pink lips, remembering our kiss in the diner, but this feels different. Permanent. Meaningful.

She doesn't move an inch, making me be the one to close the distance between us. I sink my fingers into her hair as I pull her to me. Her chest rises with a deep breath, and her eyes are trained on mine while she blinks against her bangs. I can feel her breath against my lips, and when I kiss her, hand to God, I can taste resentment on her tongue, and I will go to hell swallowing her anger like it's fucking caviar.

It's not the kiss of two newlyweds excited and eager for what's to come, but the slow, deliberate kiss of a couple exploring new territory. The way her fingers curl around the hair at the nape of my neck tells me she feels it too. Underneath all of the resentment and spite is the kindling of a fire that threatens to consume us both. She lightly bites down on my lip, pulling it with her as we pull apart, and it makes me groan.

With her eyes narrowed and so close to mine, I can see the rolling ocean in their depths. I'm a fucking prick, but that look makes me hard. There is a moment when it looks like she wants to say something, but it passes.

"Now remember there is no return to sender, and a little less conversation and a little more action can solve all your problems," Elvis interrupts while trying to grab onto my arm to get me to play along with his hip shake, but I shake it off.

Gently, I take her hand and lead her down the aisle, while Marla throws confetti into the air. Little pieces land in her hair and on the tips of her lashes, which she blinks away. Camera flashes temporarily blind me as the photographer takes pictures of us to preserve the memory.

"We'll send all the photos and the video to the email you provided," Marla says, giving us both a wide smile. She claps her hands together giddily. "You really do make a gorgeous couple," she sighs, and then steps aside so we can walk out of the chapel.

When we step into the parking lot, the breeze pushes her bangs off her forehead, and her blonde hair falls around her shoulders. I stop and look at her. She really does make a beautiful bride. Bailey holds the door to the SUV open, and before we get in, I turn to Evangeline and ask, "Have you ever been to the Eiffel Tower?"

10
Paris Syndrome

Darren

Using the private jet isn't very subtle, but I'll have to face Rausch sooner or later, and fuck if I'm flying commercial. The flight from Nevada to Virginia is only about four hours, and I check my watch before hearing the door to the bathroom where Evangeline emerges, having changed out of her wedding dress and back into her tight jeans and an oversize sweater. The smell of her perfume, floral and sweet, filters through the air as she passes by to take the seat across from me.

The stewardess refills my glass and offers Evangeline something, which she declines, and then quietly disappears back into the galley. I watch as Evangeline surveys the cabin, crossing her legs haughtily. She makes a frustrated sigh that I can't ignore. I can't ignore her *period*.

"Not to your liking?"

"You didn't waste any time spending your inheritance," she jabs. "Private jet. Very classy."

I chuckle, looking around the cabin of my *parent's* private plane.

"Feels like the inside of an expensive coffin." I shift in my seat uncomfortably.

Evangeline's eyes meet mine, a flicker of sympathy in them before it's replaced with open annoyance.

"No magazines, books, anything to pass the time?" she asks, looking around.

"If you were expecting a copy of *The Sun Also Rises,* I'm afraid you'll be disappointed," I scoff, taking a healthy sip of my drink.

"You're a pretentious asshole," she says with a bit of amusement before folding her hands in her lap.

"Why, because I prefer Hemingway to Emerson?" This debate seems to have lit a fire in her eyes. *How did someone like her become an escort?*

Almost as if she can read my thoughts, she shakes her head. "You think someone like me can't possibly be cultured?"

"I never said that."

"But you thought it, just like the woman in the dress shop," she says.

I had noticed the way the saleswoman looked at her. I had let it go the minute the woman noticed my finely cut suit and made presumptions about my wealth. That's just the way life was for me—never denied access to anything because I was wealthy. Never mind that it wasn't because of my *own* accomplishments. It wasn't even because of my father's accomplishments. The money came from my mother's family.

I open my mouth to protest, but she's not wrong. I'm rewarded with a satisfied smirk.

"Besides, I prefer *A Moveable Feast*," she says, playing

with a loose piece of string at the bottom of her sweater, and I'm a pig – an insatiable pig who's only thought is unraveling her sweater to expose what I already know is beneath it – and because I know, I want it all the more.

I'm well aware that I've only known her for a day, but I can't stop thinking about her. My heavy stare makes her cheeks turn a darker shade of pink. I rented the Paris Hotel's Eiffel Tower observatory after our wedding. I could say it was to make her happy, but selfishly, it was so I could lift the full skirt of her wedding dress to reveal the one thing that always brings me to my knees.

"So, you do love Paris." I set the glass of whiskey down and cross my arms over my chest in satisfaction.

"I never said I didn't like the city, just that I didn't want to see it." She stops playing with the string and rests her hands on either side of the arm rest.

"Ah, the Paris syndrome," I say, reminded of our conversation in the 'fake' Eiffel tower. She had explained that it's when something doesn't live up to your expectations.

Her eyes track the glass of whiskey in my hand as I take another healthy drink. She doesn't have to say anything, because I can feel her disdain. She should be glad I'm drinking, because if I weren't, I don't think I'd be as charming or as accommodating.

I already know I'm not a good person, that I drink too much, and I have yet to discover a redeeming quality about myself, but I still don't like how she looks at me.

"Would you like a drink?" I ask, ready to signal to the stewardess, but she shakes her head.

"I don't drink much," she admits.

"You're missing out," I say, turning the glass around in

my hand, the beveled crystal capturing the dim light of the cab.

She scoffs, props her chin up with the palm of her hand, and looks out the window where there's nothing but the twinkling lights of a city below.

"I know what you must think of me," I say, setting the glass down.

I roll up the sleeve of my dress shirt while propping my ankle over the opposite thigh. I didn't bother changing, except to discard my suit jacket, opting to wait until I got home.

Home.

The thought of it makes my chest tight. Not because I'm sure I'll have to face Rausch – at least maybe not today or tomorrow, but at some point soon – but because I will have to face the quiet of the hallways and picture frames holding memories.

"I don't think anything of you," she says, clear defiance in her tone, and without looking away from the window.

"Of course you do."

She turns, her critical blue eyes assessing me. I'm not sure what she sees, but I feel compelled to know, I am desperate to know exactly what she thinks, because she is unreadable and I don't like it.

"Let's not pretend that you care what I think."

I let out a breath, raising the glass of whiskey to my lips yet again. "I think you'd feel better if you just said it."

Our marriage might have been built on the foundation of revenge and spite, but at least it won't be built on lies.

"Do you want me to say that it's okay to act like a degenerate because your parents died?"

When I set the glass down rather roughly, she looks as though she wants to retract those words. The figurative band around my chest tightens a little bit more. I wanted to know, but it doesn't make it hurt any less. "You don't know me," I say tightly.

"That's right, I don't, so tell me what you so desperately want to hear." She leans forward as if she's waiting for me to speak.

I stand up from my seat and pace the cabin. "Fuck, Evan," I instinctively shorten her name like I do with Alistair's sometimes when I'm angry or frustrated. I notice her blanch as if the nickname is a gentle shake into a place she doesn't want to go.

"I know what I see," she continues, and I stop pacing as I wait for her to say something that will make me feel even worse... But her expression softens. All I see are big blue eyes peering at me with sympathy. I liked it much better when she hated me. "You're clearly in more pain than you're willing to admit," she finishes.

Running a hand through my hair, I look away.

"Wouldn't you be pissed that you had to hear about your parents' deaths from the fucking news?" I admit out loud, and then dare to look at her again. "I am so *inconsequential* to everyone on my parents' staff that no one bothered to call me!" I raise my voice, feeling pent up anger that I have no way to release. The cabin of the plane is unable to contain all the rage and grief I have contained inside.

"What about…"

"Rausch?" I cut her off, assuming she's referring to him because he showed up in my hotel the morning after, but not because he gave a shit about me. "He's the reason I'm doing this." I grab my empty glass and take it over to the bar, refilling it myself and holding a hand up to the stewardess who goes back in the galley.

Turning back around, I lean against the bar to face her. "He was going to let Lottie go," I say. "Who the fuck knows what else he's tried to do?"

"Lottie?"

"Our housekeeper," I answer. "She practically fucking raised me." I look over at Evangeline before continuing, "And before you go judging my privileged life, her family was more of a family to me than my own," I say defensively.

Evangeline is quiet and so I continue, adding softly, "I called home earlier – I didn't expect anyone to answer, but Lottie called me back. She told me that Rausch had called to talk to her about settling things with my parents' house and their staff." It was the one thing that fueled me further to go through with this. Destroying one person's life was deplorable, but I couldn't let him take the only constant person I'd ever known while growing up.

"I can understand that," she says, causing my eyes to snap over to hers.

"Rausch is not someone you want to have control over you," I say with a purposely ominous tone. "My father trusted him, and by all means, he did his job well, but sometimes…" I pause. "Sometimes I wondered who was really in office."

"I got that impression when he called me a hooker." She cocks an eyebrow. "Oh, and when he told me to go back to the corner I came from," she says with slight amusement.

"Oh, come on now." I walk over to my seat, feeling a little turbulence as the plane moves through some clouds. "I didn't think you were the kind of woman to get offended that easily."

Her black eyelashes flutter against her bangs. "A man

like Rausch wants power, but he can't get it on his own, so he has to take it from someone else."

"Is that your official diagnosis?"

"That's what I know."

I lean back in my seat and cross my legs, impressed, and unable to hide it. I'm beginning to realize that there is so much more to her than just a pretty face. "You're very observant."

"That's my job."

"I thought your job was to spread your legs?"

"Only someone simpleminded would think that. You said it yourself, *Dare*," she accentuates my shortened name, "but only part of it. Every powerful man's downfall is underestimating a woman," she says. "Even a hooker."

I can't help but laugh. "History just might prove that statement correct."

"Rausch is someone you want on your side in a political battle, but having him as an enemy is political suicide." I shake my head and sigh before looking at her when I say, "And Rausch does not like me." Which is reason enough for him to make me grovel, if not take everything away from me.

"I wonder why that is?" Evangeline asks sarcastically, tipping her chin at me.

"I've never wanted to be a politician, so I don't give a shit if he likes me or not." I smooth the wrinkles from my pants and look back up at her. She's studying me in a way someone does when they're deciding whether they trust you or not. "Besides, it's just plain fun to be the thorn in his side." I lean back into my chair, my body tired, and my mind weary. We get closer to Virginia with every mile the plane eats up, and the uneasiness in my stomach gets harder to ignore.

"I don't like you," Evangeline says with a stoic expression, "but I like Rausch even less."

Her eyes are just as tired looking as mine feel. "It's late. You should get some sleep before we arrive."

I rise from my chair, only to drop to my knees in front of her. Her eyes go wide, and I can't help but notice the thrumming pulse in her neck at my closeness. "You can recline the seat by pressing this button on the side." I lean over her, and as a result, push her thighs apart as I take hold of her hand and guide her to where the button is. She smells like cherry blossoms, which is impossible, because we're not even in Washington D.C yet and they're out of season, but still, I smell it on her skin like a phantom omen of where we're headed.

I put pressure on her finger, causing the seat to recline slowly, and watch as her breasts rise and fall with each breath under her sweater. When I decide she's reclined enough to be comfortable enough to sleep, I let go of her hand and sit back on my heels, resting my palms on the tops of her thighs. Her muscles flex beneath my hand, the way skittish horses do.

Maybe she was right when she said the downfall of a powerful man was underestimating a woman, but what a downfall it is when it's at the hand of a *beautiful* woman.

11

Queenie

Evangeline

The plane's wheels hitting the pavement jars me awake. The cabin is still dark, and when I look out the window, all I see are low brick buildings shrouded in darkness. When I move my arms to put my seat back upright, I notice a blanket covering me. I can tell it's not a regular airplane blanket because of the soft, beautifully woven fabric. Across from me, Darren is resting in his seat, his suit jacket draped over his chest. When our eyes meet, he looks away, adjusting his seat to gather his things.

I'm pretty sure Darren was the one to put the blanket on me. I want to say something but the words feel stuck in my throat, and the plane coming to a stop forces them back down.

Looking out the window one more time, I can see there's a hint of the rising sun through the midnight-blue sky. Raising my arms above my head, I take a big stretch and find my body still stiff. I couldn't have been asleep for more than a couple of hours, but everything protests when I unclip my seatbelt and stand up.

"Welcome to Virginia, Mrs. Walker," the stewardess's voice interrupts my thoughts as she smiles at me. It takes my brain a few moments to recognize the name. Fidgeting with the dice ring on my finger, I can't help but chuckle a little remembering the look on Darren's face when he realized he'd forgotten rings. The ring's a tad too big for my finger, it slides easily around, allowing me to use it as distraction. I smile at her and grab my purse but notice Darren smirking at me. Embarrassed that he'd caught me reminiscing about the ring, I lift my middle finger to him.

The stewardess shows me to the door where we disembark, but when I look back to make sure Darren is behind me, I see he's folding the blanket carefully before he leaves it on the seat.

A black sedan idles next to the plane. When we get to the car, Bailey opens the door for me, and I realize he must have disembarked before us. Darren slides in next to me, and I notice the dark circles under his eyes. I don't think he got much sleep on the plane, not that the few short hours I got did any good for me. I almost feel worse, and though my body craves sleep, it craves caffeine even more.

"My luggage?" I ask, looking around to see who's taking care of it, because I don't even know where it was being stowed.

"Taken care of," he says quietly, crossing his ankle over his thigh, leaning back into the soft leather seat.

Everything seems to run so stealthily, from Bailey embarking and disembarking without being seen, to the stewardess showing up to provide something I didn't even know I wanted, to the waiting car we're sitting in. My luggage seems to have been swallowed up in this magic trick where everything appears just when you need it.

The car pulls away from the plane and out of the airport. I look out the window as dawn crests the horizon, a bright orange that bleeds into the sky like a watercolor painting. Darren tips his head back, and a soft sigh escapes his lips as if he's releasing all of the tension he's been holding onto the whole plane ride. In his lap, he plays with the gold watch on his wrist in the same way I fidget with the dice on my finger.

The watch doesn't even work. The large hand is stuck at twelve when I know it's almost morning. I look back up at his face and notice his eyes are closed, long black lashes barely cresting the top of his cheeks, but he's not sleeping because his thumb still brushes over the face of the watch.

I turn again to look out my window and see the outline of a city I've never been to as we cross the Potomac. I'm ashamed to admit to myself but I've looked up the Washington neighborhoods on the map so that I could see what the streets and the houses looked like, and now that I'm here, crossing over into Washington DC, my skin feels like tiny ants are crawling over me at the wrongness of the situation. I have the overwhelming urge to run, but I can't – I can't run, because I want to know – I want to see the house where Kerry Walker lived.

THE CAR PULLS through a sleepy neighborhood lined with maple trees that look as though they've caught fire – deep golds and reds on display like the rising sun. Rusty red-brick Federalist style houses appear, set far back from the sidewalks with deep, lush lawns. We stop in front of a large home with a white pillared front porch.

Bailey opens my door, and Darren meets me in front of the walkway, but he doesn't go in right away. Instead, he stands there looking at the door as if he expects someone to open it and greet him.

I can't imagine what's going through his mind, and I shouldn't care, but I try to lighten the mood by asking, "What? No staff to open the door for you?"

He snaps out of his trance and a smile spreads across his face. "I'm not as pretentious as you think, Queenie," he replies while we walk up the steps.

"I doubt that," I tease back as he unlocks the door and opens it while I trail behind him. "Queenie? As in what Emerson called his second wife?"

"Of course."

"I don't like it."

He smiles. "All the better."

Bailey walks in behind us, rolling our luggage into the foyer, and then he disappears before I can even say thank you.

"Are you thirsty?" he asks.

I hadn't realized I was until he asked. "Yes."

Darren grabs our luggage and walks past the stairs and towards the back of the house.

"My parents…" he pauses, taking a minute as he collects himself. "They always have water stocked in the fridge."

I follow him further into the house, passing by artwork and framed family photos on the white walls, admiring the beautiful wainscoting, something that reminds me of pictures in an architectural magazine. There's a formal living room, and across from it, there's another room with a grand piano and fireplace. I wonder if any of them played, or if it was just for decoration.

The home looks old, its history carefully preserved but updated to fit modern living. I pass a large staircase with a light wood railing which I presume leads up to the bedrooms.

Darren enters the kitchen, where white-veined marble countertops and immaculately clean appliances look as though no one has ever cooked in this house. On the counter is an expensive looking espresso machine that looks like it belongs in a trendy coffee shop instead of someone's home. Darren looks at it with trepidation but then opens the refrigerator, grabs two water bottles, and hands one to me.

He shoves the luggage inside a door off the kitchen while I look at the espresso machine with longing while downing the water.

He leans against the kitchen island, and the silence seems to swallow us whole. Darren's rumpled shirt and wrinkled pants make him seem out of place in this pristine kitchen, but then maybe he's always been out of place in a home like this. Everything is decorated in either cream or white, and the architecture screams old money with no room for sticky hands or dirty faces.

I can't picture Darren growing up in a place like this. It looks more like a museum than a home. He runs a hand through his hair as he looks around the kitchen, his eyes settling on the back window that I notice looks out to a beautiful garden.

I stand behind him as he places his hands on the large farmhouse sink and hangs his head. "Are you okay?" I ask, raising my hand to place on his shoulder, but I lower it before making contact.

Darren tilts his head towards me like he wants to say something, but then he closes his mouth, turning away from the garden, his demeanor shifting.

"I need to wash my fucking clothes," he says, pushing open the door off the kitchen to reveal the laundry room which looks bigger than my bedroom back in my apartment in Vegas. He proceeds to dump the contents of his bag into a nearby basket with force.

"Wow, you could have a whole servant's quarters in here. Where's the cot?"

Darren glares at me. "Boy, you don't hide your disdain for wealth, and yet you accepted five-million dollars from me."

"*Accepted* is not really the word I would use," I grit out through my teeth.

I stand with my arms crossed over my chest, watching as he continues to try and figure out how to use the washing machine – and failing miserably.

"Why is this shit so fucking hard?" he growls, randomly turning dials and pressing buttons with no success, and I can't help but enjoy his frustration.

"I would ask if you had someone who does your laundry, but I don't want to get my head bitten off again," I say.

He turns and glares at me. "Lottie doesn't come until Monday," he grumbles.

I sniff while leaning against the door jamb, my arms crossed over my chest as I watch him struggle.

I almost feel sorry for him—almost. He gives me a pleading look. "If you were planning on doing laundry at some point, could you throw some of mine in there?"

I pick up one of his shirts, looking at the tag. "Hmm, it's not made with *rayon*," I say sarcastically, "so I don't think I know how to wash it." I toss it back in the basket angrily.

"Jesus, are you ever going to act civil?" he responds.

I balk. "You want civil, you should have married one of your Cotillion dates."

There's a flare in his hazel eyes, the green burning brighter and taking over the brown. He stands close to me when he says, "If I wanted a debutante, I would have bought one."

I look at the basket of laundry, and then back at him. "You want me to do your laundry?"

He steps away and looks at me with skepticism. "Yeah?"

"Is that a question or an answer?"

"It would be helpful," he says with trepidation.

I smile. "Consider it a favor."

12
Give All to Love

Evangeline

With my hair still damp, I throw on an oversized t-shirt and pad down the hall towards the stairs in my bare feet. I'd only intended to take a nap, but the hall is cast in the early evening's dim light, making it seem cold and lonely. Along the walls are framed pictures of Darren at various ages, photographed with his parents. Some look as though they are from vacations they took, and others are posed family portraits. I stop and stare at one taken during his father's campaign. Darren is sitting at one of the desks with a phone to his ear, looking like he doesn't want to be there by the glare in his eyes while his father is standing nearby, talking to his wife. I feel this pang in my chest that shouldn't be there. They looked happy, even amongst the chaos of the campaign going on around them.

I have to tear my eyes away from the photo to continue down the stairs. The house is larger than it looks from the outside, with long hallways and more rooms than needed for a family of three. There are several rooms upstairs, but they were all closed and dark, meaning Darren didn't sleep in any of them, which leaves me to wonder if he slept at all.

My bare feet are silent against the hardwood floors as I step off the last stair, and I find myself standing outside of Senator Kerry Walker's office.

From the outside, his office looks completely different from the rest of the house, decorated with dark walnut, green textured wallpaper, and a deep leather couch. When I push the door open wider, I notice the set of bookshelves that line the wall, and I can't stop myself from stepping over the threshold and into a room I probably shouldn't be in. I tell myself that it's wrong, but I imagine it smells like him – like the spines of old books and leather. The bookcases go all the way to the ceiling, and there are so many with their different colored spines lined perfectly on the shelves, as if they are begging to be touched.

I'm not sure if the books are organized in any sort of way, so I work my way from left to right, my finger running over gold embossed spines, and others that look well-loved and used, stopping on *The Collective Works of Ralph Waldo Emerson.* I'm almost afraid to touch it, but I pull it out anyway, turning it over in my hand, knowing that he, too, held this book, and it's as if the memory I have of him has become tangible. The spine is worn and cracked, one of the well-used and well-loved books in what must be a collection of thousands.

From behind me, I hear Darren's voice, rough and quiet as he recites the ending verse of Emerson's poem, *Give All To Love*.

Though thou loved her as thyself,

As a self of purer clay,
Though her parting dims the day,
Stealing grace from all alive;
Heartily know,
When half-gods go,
The gods arrive.

I slip the book back into its place. I wanted to tell him that I knew his father once, but it was a secret that I wanted to keep close—something that was just mine and no one else's, like a treasured timepiece. There never seemed to be a right time, and I wouldn't expect Darren to understand that after only meeting Kerry once, he had an impact that would stay with me for years. But I can't tell him now, especially when I'm standing in his office, holding his book.

I turn around to see Darren in the doorway, wearing a faded Georgetown t-shirt that looks as though it's been washed one too many times and is possibly a size too small for him now. He looks like a frat boy with his lean figure, the shirt fitting tight across his broad chest, and jeans that sit low on his waist. His hair looks freshly washed, the ends still wet and messy. The dark circles under his eyes are gone, but not the shadow they cast.

"For someone who claims to dislike Emerson, you sure have quite the catalog memorized," I say, moving away from the bookcase and focusing my attention on the artwork lining the other wall as the oriental rug in front of the desk warms my bare feet. Fall in Washington D.C. is much colder than in Nevada. I have to remember to wear socks.

"I never said I disliked Emerson," Darren returns as he pushes off the door frame and walks into the office. He looks as though he's treading carefully, shoving his hands in the pockets of his jeans as if expecting someone to catch him in a place he shouldn't be. Then I'm reminded that *I'm* the intruder.

When we'd first arrived, Darren had made a point to say that I could make myself at home and to help myself to anything before he showed me the guest room upstairs. I didn't take that to mean I could enter his father's private office though.

"I was passing by – the door was open, and I saw the…"

"Books," he finishes for me, the corners of his mouth tugging into a reluctant smile.

"Yes," I say quietly, pushing a piece of hair behind my ear. "I'm sorry, I shouldn't have come in here," I apologize while walking towards the door.

He steps in front of me, grabbing my waist, his hand warm and firm through the shirt. "Stay," he says, tilting his head towards me. The green flecks in his eyes glimmer in the low light of an antique lamp next to us. "I like seeing you in here," he admits, although I'm not sure what he means by that, so I stay.

"Okay," I reply, trying to navigate this space which means different things to both of us.

Perhaps it's Darren's way of facing his demon's while I simply give into mine.

"My father would hate it," Darren says, a touch of wicked amusement in his voice.

Maybe I should be offended that Darren thinks that someone like me – someone who has fucked men for money – wouldn't be welcome, but that makes it all the more enticing. The way Darren is watching me make my way around the office leads me believe he feels the same way.

I turn my attention to the desk and run my hand along the edge of the dark walnut, feeling the wood graze my skin. A pen lays on top of a leather-bound pad of legal paper, as if waiting for him to come back to jot down a private thought.

"It's a beautiful office," I say, leaning over the desk to look at the framed poem on the wall, the same poem Darren recited in the bar while drunk.

Darren grunts behind me, the noise sounding as though it's coming from low in his throat.

"You don't think so?" I ask, turning my head to look at him.

Darren drops his arms to his sides and moves behind me. "It loses its grandeur when you only come in here to get lectured or yelled at."

I haven't decided if I should feel sorry for him or not, but the way his body feels against my back and the wood of the desk against my palms clouds my judgment. I can picture Darren standing in front of this desk, hands in his pockets, staring past his father to the framed poem on the wall while being reprimanded by something foolish he did.

Maybe I'm drawn to tragedy… the same way I was drawn into the office of a man I once knew, and the same way I'm drawn to Darren. They are a lot alike, but different in so many ways.

The first time I heard the Emerson poem, *Give All To Love*, I was sitting in a literature class. The teacher was reciting it from a book. We were analyzing the words, inferring what Emerson intended, and I couldn't wrap my head around it. Emerson was dead – how could we possibly know the meaning if we couldn't ask him? I couldn't grasp the concept at the time. And it wasn't until the second time I heard the poem—when Kerry Walker recited it at the University of Arizona—that I understood Emerson's words. I could feel them deep in my bones, awakening something inside of me that I never knew was there.

"He wrote it for his wife who died," I explain as Darren moves to the side. "The poem," I remind him when I see the question in his eyes as I turn around, resting my hip against the desk.

He runs a hand through his hair, the strands now almost dry, and nods as if he's taking my word for it.

I pinch my brows together. "You memorized the words, but you don't know the meaning?"

He laughs softly. "I had an English lit teacher that made us memorize poems."

"In college?" I ask curiously, raising my hand to touch the Georgetown emblem on his shirt, the material soft but his chest hard underneath.

"Boarding school." He shrugs with a coy smile.

Of course he went to boarding school. "And you still remember the poems?" For someone who seems indifferent about Emerson, or *anything* for that matter, he's held those words captive, close to his heart, all this time. If he didn't care about them, perhaps he would have forgotten them a long time ago. That just makes Darren all the more of an enigma to me.

"I remember *too* many things," he says, cryptically.

"Sounds like a curse – not being able to forget things." I grip the edge of the desk while Darren moves to stand in front of me once again, his hands resting heavily on my hips, pulling a sigh from me.

"It raises expectations that I'd rather stay low," he admits with a sexy smirk.

His messy brown hair falls over his forehead, him having run his hand through it too many times. I drag my fingers along his jaw, feeling the light stubble he's let grow in – either on purpose, or because loss has made it near impossible to have the will to shave. Either way, I like the way the roughness feels against my fingers, and my stomach tightens at the thought of what it would feel like against my thighs.

"Your father wouldn't like me in here?" I ask, lifting an eyebrow.

Darren's hands grip my waist harder.

"No," he rasps as his thumbs rub along my hip bones.

"Why is that?" I ask, looking up at him through my bangs.

I can see the heat in his eyes, the green flecks swallowed up into huge black pools of need. "He wouldn't approve of your profession," Darren answers, wetting his lips as I place my hands on his chest, feeling his hard muscles underneath.

"Hmm, a politician with morals," I say, cocking my head to the side while moving my hand down his chest towards the waistband of his jeans. "So he wouldn't approve of me doing this?" I turn away from Darren and lean over the corner of the desk to reach for the pen while I run the center of my pussy along the hard wood. I rock my hips high in the air to give Darren a very provocative view as the wood digs deep into my panties, along my center, and hits the apex where my clit becomes sensitive, causing me to suck in a breath.

Looking over my shoulder, I can see Darren watching me with rapt attention. His eyes are on my ass while I rock back and forth, the action causing my shirt to ride up, exposing the creamy white of my panties – the pen now long discarded.

"Jesus," Darren groans from behind me, the little pulse in his neck ticking like a time bomb. His teeth dig into his lip when I pick up the cadence, and his hand curls into a fist at his side.

"Or do you think he'd want to watch?" I continue the game, closing my eyes as I move my hips up and down, pushing my ass further into the air as the friction of the rounded corner causes the sensations to heighten. Long, laborious strokes – each time it passes over my clit my breath hitches, and I hear Darren's strangled groan from behind me.

I know that what I'm doing is shameful and absurdly obscene, fucking the desk that used to belong to Senator Kerry Walker while his son watches, but that's why it feels so good. This room is filled with his presence – in the spines of each book, in the scratches on the desk, and even hidden inside the words of the Emerson poem that hangs on the wall. If Darren wants to use me to get back at his father, then I might as well give him his money's worth.

Letting my hair hang over my face, swaying back and forth against the desk, I rub harder, a bolt of unthinkable desire sparking inside of me, cut short by Darren grabbing onto my hips and spinning me around. He pushes me against the desk roughly, his hand resting at the base of my neck, holding me in place. I'm not sure whether he's going to curse me or fuck me.

"You are a very wicked girl," he rasps with a voice that sounds like torn paper.

I smile, blink up at him, and wrap my arms around his

shoulders. He lifts me onto the desk, spreading my legs as his body settles against me.

His mouth hovers over mine, and I can smell the sweet caramel scent of whiskey.

"You have no idea, husband," I say, parting my lips and feeling the pressure of his cock against me, so hard and so ready.

He grins his approval and runs his hands under my shirt, lifting it over my head, tossing it carelessly to the floor. I shake out my hair, feeling it fall against my bare back, the coldness of the room causing my nipples to immediately turn to tiny points that rub against the lettering of his shirt, sending a spark of desire down my spine.

He tilts me back to pull one of my nipples into his mouth, and I moan in response. I'm already so sensitive everywhere with the need to come.

I suck in a breath, arching my back for him to take more, and it sends a desperate ache through me, like adding lighter fluid to an already burning fire. My hand slides out from under me; a container of pens crash to the floor.

"It's going to feel so good to fuck you on my father's desk." Darren tugs me closer, his mouth hot and eager against my skin as he makes his way back up to my mouth, and I want it, I want him to fuck me so bad that my cunt aches, wet and needy.

I grab onto the ends of his shirt, and we break apart momentarily so I can pull it over his head before his mouth crashes against mine again, his tongue licking inside while he pulls my thigh around his waist. It's the inappropriateness that fuels the urgency; the way something so wrong can make you light up on the inside like nothing else can.

"What do you think he would say if he knew what you were going to do to me?" I ask breathlessly while pulling at the button of his jeans, popping it open so I can lower the zipper while his mouth finds my breasts again. He's so hard that the top of his cock is settled against his stomach, peaking over the waistband of his briefs, the dusky head glistening with pre-cum. I grab him roughly, pulling him towards me, and Darren hisses in response. He releases me long enough to grab a condom from his pocket and pushes his jeans further down.

"He would say that I was wasting my talents on fucking a woman I have no future with." His mouth moves down my body, and I tip my head back in a lust induced haze.

He tugs at my panties, and I lift my hips so he can pull them down in a hurry. The action is quick, and I'm already so wet that he slides into me easily, thrusting so hard he practically lifts me off the desk. A whoosh of air escapes my lungs as I wrap my arms around his waist and hold on.

He pushes me harder into the desk, and I arch my back as thrust after thrust brings me to a place where no thoughts can invade my mind, just the feeling of complete submission. When his thumb grazes my clit, I'm so sensitive that it threatens to send me through the roof and my body bucks against him. His thumb continues to circle and rub with the same cadence as his cock moving inside me, and I catch myself mewling.

"Don't stop, no one can hear you but me," he breathes, and I moan, not because he gave me permission, but because it frees me, and I give him everything.

"God, you feel so fucking good," he bites out, which elicits another moan from me.

I *want* to feel good. I *want* to be the one who sends him over the edge, but his thumb presses hard, circling faster, and I can't stop the butterflies that cause my stomach and thighs to tremble in response, an involuntary reaction I have no control over. My impending orgasm is so close that I beg for it.

In return, he picks up his pace, sweat glistening on his brow while the feverish look in his eyes threatens to turn me to ash. I'm sent over the edge; the orgasm is sharp as it twists and turns around my spine as I pant and gasp. Darren is close, his breathing ragged and his movements fierce.

Suddenly he pulls out and turns me over so that I'm bent over the desk. Everything on the desk crashes to the floor. My palms press into the desk, my breasts push hard into the wood, feeling each sliver as he pushes inside me from behind, grabbing onto my hips to pull me into him with each thrust.

"You look absolutely fucking perfect bent over my father's desk," he grits out deliberately, causing my stomach to tighten again, my cunt still pulsing. I can't help the reaction. Some deep-seated feelings rush to the surface as either another orgasm begins to build, or the last one is still fighting its way through me.

As Darren fucks his demons away, I sink into mine.

I dig my fingers into the wooden desk as I stare at the Emerson poem hanging on the wall while Darren fucks me from behind.

13

Georgetown T-Shirt

Darren

The couch in the formal living room is the only place that doesn't bring up memories, and that's probably because we never used it. Furniture from the seventeenth century isn't meant to be very comfortable; it's meant to look pretentiously expensive. I've been sitting here for the better part of the evening, unable to sleep, and now that the sun is starting to come up, the drink in my hand seems less desirable. If I'm being completely honest, it was less desirable when the sun went *down*.

When the doorbell rings, I'm startled out of my thoughts. Rising from the couch, I leave my drink on the antique table and walk down the hall to the foyer. On either side of the double doors are frosted glass panels, and I can see the outline of someone—someone familiar—which is the only reason I open the door.

Alistair barges in. "Dare," he says, looking at me. "Where have you been? I've called you about a hundred times."

Instead of going back into the living room, I walk down the hall towards the kitchen, Alistair following me like an angry puppy.

"I turned my phone off."

"You didn't come home. I was worried," he says a little sheepishly.

"Well, if you suspected I was cheating on you, don't worry," I pause, "I was." I smirk to avoid what we both know is a touchy subject.

We weren't each others' keepers, that's for sure. Disappearing for some time was the norm for both of us, although these circumstances are different, and we both know it.

"Very funny. But while you were on the private jet, I was flying commercial," he argues.

"What a travesty, having to fly first class. I'm so sorry," I say sarcastically, turning towards the refrigerator to grab some leftovers when the smell of coffee distracts me. It's not just *any* coffee, it's the expensive kind my mother loves. Lottie doesn't start back until Monday, so it wasn't her. The only other person who could have used the espresso machine was Evangeline and—I look over at the counter—she didn't leave me a cup.

Fuck.

I slam the refrigerator door closed and find Alistair leaning against the island staring at me. "You didn't happen to bring coffee, did you?" I ask.

Alistair smacks me in the head. "You know I don't drink coffee."

I slump into the barstool and rub my head while glaring at him. "You went to that trendy shop around the corner from our apartment like every day for weeks."

"I was trying to get into the barista's pants, and once I

did," he shrugs, "well, there was no more reason to go back."

"You are a debased human being," I accuse him, leaning my forehead against my palm.

Alistair clears his throat. "I'm not the one who got a girl fired so she would marry you," he says in an accusatory tone.

I stand up, pushing the chair back roughly. "Fuck off, Alistair," I spit, about to walk away when I see Evangeline standing in the doorway of the kitchen. She's wearing my Georgetown t-shirt, and *fuck* if I don't like the way it looks on her.

After I fucked her in my father's office, we spent the evening eating takeout while standing in the kitchen, and I gave her my shirt to wear. I'm not a decent person – nobody knows this more than me, but in this instance, I do have the decency to look remorseful at the exchange she probably overheard.

Just when I thought maybe we were past that and on our way to some sort of civility…

Alistair looks at me with a petulant smile, and then, schooling his face, looks back at Evangeline.

"I wish I could say it was a pleasure seeing you again, Alistair, but it's not," she says, narrowing her eyes at him, and I can't help but suppress a smirk.

"Fair enough," Alistair concedes.

Evangeline walks into the kitchen with an espresso cup in hand. She saunters past and over to the espresso machine. Grabbing the grounds from a nearby cabinet she starts up the machine, pressing the beans, and goddammit if she makes fucking steam. When she's finished, she turns around and brings the steaming cup to her mouth and I visibly salivate.

I look to see if, by a slim chance, she made two.

"You didn't make me…"

"No," she cuts me off.

"Well, can you at least show me…"

"No," she cuts me off again, and Alistair, that motherfucker, starts laughing.

I turn and glare at him while Evangeline hops up on the counter, dangling those fucking perfect legs of hers while she drinks her coffee.

"Somebody fucking shoot me right now."

"I don't like guns, but I'd gladly smack you in the head if that's what you want," she says through the steam rising off her cup.

Alistair raises a hand. "Already taken care of," he says with a smile, and Evangeline rolls her eyes.

"So, Alistair, use any more of your connections," she uses air quotes, "to track down another hooker lately?"

I'm jealous that those eyes are directed at Alistair, the pale blues flaring with anger. Her anger should be reserved for me.

Alistair holds up his hands. "Look, I just came here to check on Dare," he professes, "but it looks like you got everything handled," he addresses me with a raised brow.

Evangeline scoffs, the sound more like a kitten than a lion. Alistair pushes off from the counter, pulls his phone out and holds it out to me.

"My parents got this," he says, somberly.

I hold the phone in my hand and read the announcement regarding the funeral. There's a service at the Congressional Cathedral for friends and family, and then a private burial at the National Cemetery.

I drop the phone back in Alistair's hand.

"I wasn't sure if you got it," he says, placing the phone

back in his pocket, "seeing how you don't like to check your phone."

Rubbing the back of my neck, I turn away from him and face the window that looks out to my mother's garden. I'm sure my father's office has provided details about the service; I just haven't wanted to see it. I have a couple of days to get myself together, though, because sooner rather than later, I will have to face this.

"Just call me if you need me," Alistair says. "I'll see you on Sunday."

Evangeline is still in the kitchen, her feet dangling off the counter as she looks at me somberly. "Do you have a black dress?" I ask.

She narrows her eyes. "Yes."

Placing my hands in my pockets, I stand awkwardly in front of her, studying her face, the smattering of freckles across the tops of her cheeks, the arch of her eyebrows, and the clear blue of her eyes as she seems to look right into me. It's unnerving, but I suppose I'm not hiding things very well, and what do I care if she knows how I feel?

My fucking parents died and I'm in their kitchen, worrying about coffee and imagining my *wife*, who happens to be an escort, naked on top of the goddamn counter. She looks good in my Georgetown t-shirt, and my dad would be so fucking pissed because he paid for my education, only for me to pass on taking the bar. Well, *fuck* all that now.

The chill in the room causes me to shiver, and I remember I had some shirts in the laundry room, so I open the door to find a stack of clothes sitting on the counter. When I grab one of the shirts, I notice a hole in it.

"What the fuck?" I grab another one, and it's cut up

the side. I start sifting through the other shirts which all have either a hole or a cut. Even my fucking underwear has holes in them—strategically placed.

"Evangeline!" I yell out the door and look around the corner to find her gone. "Jesus fucking Christ!" I throw the pile of clothes in the trash, a bubble of angry laughter threatening to spill over.

14

Souvenir from Vegas

Evangeline

Padding into the kitchen in search of something to eat, I open the fridge and survey its contents. It isn't well stocked, but there's leftovers and snacks. I select a bowl of grapes and wash them in the sink while looking out the window to the garden – the same garden I noticed Darren looking at the other day after Alistair showed him the email about his parents' services.

I'd assumed since he asked if I had a black dress that I was going to accompany him, and I'm apprehensive because I don't think it's my place. I hadn't been to a funeral since my grandfather died, and that had been so long ago. His was a simple service at a funeral home, not at a hundred-year-old cathedral. The only flag that was flown at half-mast for my grandfather's funeral was the one at the VFW hall in town, not at every government building in the Washington D.C. area.

As I look out at the rose garden, only a few stems still remain, but what a magnificent garden it must have been in the summer. Finding a bowl in one of the cabinets, I place the grapes inside and then hop up on the countertop, and begin to pluck a few off the stems.

"Well, I see now what has Darren so preoccupied," Rausch says, startling me.

His large presence leeches into the kitchen, charging the once neutral space where Darren and I have shared takeout and light conversation.

The house has been empty, too much space for only two people to occupy, but I didn't expect anyone else to enter it, especially not Rausch.

Underneath his dark blue suit and perfectly knotted red and blue striped tie, he seems to bristle with agitated energy. I don't think he was expecting to find me here. Maybe he didn't think Darren would go through with it, or maybe he already knows and just wants to irritate me.

The problem isn't that he's here – because that seemed inevitable – the problem is that I'm not wearing anything besides a pair of boy shorts and knee-high socks.

I can't help but notice the moment when his eyes land on my bare breasts. The tick in his jaw tells me it affects him, but how, I'm not sure. I'm not embarrassed. I know exactly who I am, and I don't hide from it. I can tell Rausch is marginally embarrassed, at least enough to look away.

Instead of trying to cover myself, I pluck another grape from the bowl next to me as I sit on the counter, letting my socked feet dangle. This isn't my house, but it isn't Rausch's either. "I would say it's nice to see you again, but…" I leave the rest of the sentence to sit in the charged air between us.

He digs a finger into the knot of his tie, loosening it as if to aid in being able to breathe. His agitation seems to work its way like a snake over the countertops and through the cabinets. There's not enough history between us to justify his hostility, but since I'm the only other person in the room, the anger seems to be directed towards me.

"Darren's brought home a souvenir from Vegas." He enters the kitchen further, placing his fingertips on the kitchen island. He seems familiar, like he's spent more time in this home than his own, the way he walked right in without pause. The large slab of white marble is the only object that separates us.

I smile and plop another grape into my mouth. "A very *expensive* souvenir," I say, arching an eyebrow.

He makes a noise deep in his throat, but his facial expression remains stoic, as if me sitting on the counter with my breasts exposed is inconsequential. Rausch does not seem to be the type of man who would take advantage of a woman, even a topless one swinging her socked feet like a schoolgirl in front of him. Something tells me he wouldn't *have* to take advantage of a woman, because his presence alone exudes power and confidence. Rausch is a controlled enigma that I have yet to figure out, but I'm not sure I want to.

I don't know much about Rausch, other than he ran Senator Walker's office: the man behind the veil, pulling the strings in American politics - *the kingmaker,* as Darren so ominously referred to him. I've met my fair share of prominent figures, and I doubt any of them remember meeting me, but Rausch doesn't look like he forgets a face.

"Do you have a habit of walking around naked in someone else's house?" he asks disapprovingly.

"I'm not naked," I counter while kicking out a socked foot and looking down at my panties.

He sniffs loudly. "Do you know whose house this is?" he demands.

"Darren Walker's."

He uses his large hand to rub his sharp chin – his eyes lingering on me as if he's trying to figure me out. If Darren had not announced that I was his fiancée in Vegas, I doubt he would think twice about me now. Perhaps I'd be just one of the many women in and out of Darren's bed.

Chuckling darkly, he says, "This," he motions around, "is not *Darren's* house." He grits his teeth.

I should grab a shirt and call for Darren – but where's the fun in that? Rausch is so tightly wound that the sight of my breasts, or just my presence, threatens to unravel him.

"You're right, it's our house," I say to piss him off.

Hopping off the counter, I grab the bowl of grapes. Rausch presses a hand against the refrigerator door above my head.

His large body presses close to mine – so close that his tie skims my nipple, causing the already tightened bud to send a shiver into my stomach. I look up through my bangs to see the corners of his mouth pull into a smile and I feel the table turn.

"Don't *fuck* with me little girl," he says in a low tone. "I don't know *who* you think you are—"

"My *wife*," I hear Darren's threatening voice declare from behind Rausch.

"I didn't think you'd actually go through with it," Rausch chuckles darkly.

I certainly wasn't expecting him to laugh, but somehow, that makes it worse. When the laughter subsides, there's an eerie silence in the kitchen.

"I might be a degenerate, but at least I'm one that keeps his promises," Darren says, walking further into the room.

"This is fucking ridiculous," Rausch sneers, throwing his hands in the air as if someone has just played a trick on him. "What did you expect, Darren? Marry a hooker, get your money, and you're rid of me?"

I don't think he's expecting an answer.

"Pretty much," Darren says defiantly, crossing his arms over his chest.

Rausch lowers his head so he can pinch the bridge of his nose. I should leave, but my feet feel frozen to the spot, and I can't look away. Besides, I don't want to leave Darren.

"I shouldn't be shocked by your behavior because you've always been a fuckup, but this…" he tilts his head in my direction and shakes his head again. The disappointment leaks off him and seeps into the space between the three of us.

Darren straightens his back, his broad shoulders stretching the gray t-shirt across his chest. His face is strained as if he's trying hard not to react, because reacting is what Rausch wants.

"You're pissed because you don't have control anymore," Darren challenges him.

"Do you not get it, Darren? Not everything is about you. Your parents are dead."

The minute he says it, Darren blanches, his eyes growing wide, and all the air is expelled from his lungs. "You don't think I know that?" Darren explodes, and I think he might punch Rausch, but instead, Darren reaches behind his head and pulls his shirt off and hands it to me. I look down at the shirt and take it from him, his hand lingering a moment longer, his fingers grazing mine. Gratefully, I slip it on.

"My father might have trusted you to handle things, but I don't," Darren's voice is steady and less combative than earlier.

"That's laughable coming from someone who couldn't even take the Bar," Rausch says.

Darren narrows his eyes. "Couldn't and wouldn't are two *very* different things."

I get the feeling this is a very old argument between them.

"When are you gonna grow up, Darren?" Rausch asks rhetorically. "Your father had plans for you." His voice softens.

"His plans, not mine," Darren says, defensively.

In dissatisfaction, Rausch places his hands in his pockets. His face is still etched with disappointment. "This is your mess now. Don't expect me to clean it up for you," he says, and then exits the kitchen, leaving us alone.

Darren closes the few feet distance between us. "I'm sorry about that," he says genuinely while his hands run down both my arms, his eyes roaming over me as if to inspect for damage.

"I know how to handle a man like Rausch," I say, but I'm not sure I even convince myself.

"I'm sure you can," he says with a glint of amusement in his eyes.

"Thank you for the shirt."

He leans in close, brushing his lips near my ear, and I can smell his cologne; like carelessness and pine trees.

"Just be glad it wasn't one of the ones with *fucking* holes in them," he growls, and my body stiffens.

"Well, thank God for little miracles." I inch my way around him and head for the coffee machine.

"Those were expensive shirts, Evangeline."

"I'm sure you can buy new ones."

Darren scratches the back of his head. "How about a truce?" he offers, and I tilt my head, listening. "Do you think you can behave for my parent's funeral?"

I set the cup down and grip the edge of the counter behind me. "I'm not a dog, Darren. Of course I can behave."

"So then we're even?"

"Not by a long shot."

15
My Wife

Darren

I get out of the car before Bailey has a chance to open the door, and then I lean down, holding my hand out for Evangeline. One leg extends from the car, placing a high heeled foot on the pavement, and as she looks up at me with wide eyes, I grab hold of her hand to help her out.

The sky looks bleak and gray as clouds descend, threatening to rain. Of course it would rain today. We stand at the curb in front of the white bricked spires of the Washington National Cathedral. The imposing gothic-style church has held the services for many Senators, and now fills with mourners for my parents, Senator Kerry Walker, and Merrill Compton-Walker.

Would my mother get such a lavish service if she hadn't died along with my father? Thinking about it would only lead me down a rabbit hole that I don't have enough whiskey in my flask to fill. Taking a sip, I place it back in the inside pocket of my coat. Evangeline adjusts the belt on her jacket, and then grabs hold of my hand. At the steps of the Cathedral are the press, waiting like vultures to get pictures of who's showing up like it's a fucking red-carpet affair.

Evangeline starts to walk but I hold her back, and she gives me a confused look. To my left, behind the barricade fence is a familiar man.

"Is everything okay?" Evangeline asks, and normally it's a question that would seem ignorant under the circumstances, because of course everything is *not* okay, but she follows my gaze as an older man pushes through the barricade and approaches us.

For a moment I'm taken off guard, not sure what to expect.

The more I look at him, the more familiar he seems, and I feel like I should know him, but I don't. I study his face, the same wide eyes and thin nose. I realize the last time I saw this man was when I was in the fifth grade.

It was the only time I ever recall my father yelling so loudly that I could hear him in my second-floor bedroom. I stood outside my father's office, looking through the crack in the door to see him arguing with someone. It was the desperation and hurt in his voice that made me realize my father wasn't unbreakable.

Even when he'd been tackling a difficult court case, I'd never seen him this visibly upset. To describe him as passionate during his campaign was an understatement, and certainly when I'd started acting out, he still wasn't as upset as he was that night. His foul mood had lasted for weeks.

My eleven-year-old self had nearly been knocked over by this man when he'd burst out of my father's office. Once he realized who I was, the anger in his face slowly dissolved. He didn't introduce himself, but he didn't have to, because even at the age of eleven, I could see the resemblance between him and my father. All he did was touch the top of my head, and then he was gone, never to be seen again.

My father was one of four boys, and the only one to ever go to college. He didn't speak to his family, and I'd never seen my uncles or grandparents, nor did my father ever speak of them. My father wasn't born, he just *was*. At least that was how my eleven-year-old self thought of him.

Now at the age of twenty-seven, here he stood in front of me again, with that same softened expression that seemed reserved just for this moment – just for me. He was older, frailer than I remember. This man doesn't belong here, my father wouldn't have wanted him here – and there is a part of me that wants to honor my father's wishes.

"Darren?" he asks.

The cold and wet morning has seemed to have temporarily absconded with my voice, and when I don't answer he asks, "Do you know who I am?"

"I know who you are."

"Then your father told you about me," he says, in a hopeful tone.

"You should leave."

His face falls slightly as if whatever hope he had was just wiped away. I feel Evangeline squeeze my hand tighter, making me aware that we are standing in front of the church where my parents' service is being held, and I can't deal with this – not here.

"That was my son," he raises his voice, garnering the attention of those nearby. "I had to hear about it in the paper. Do you know what that's like?" he asks, unaware of the parallel between us making my body tight, like the stretch of a rubber band about to break.

"You don't have a son," Rausch interrupts, motioning for security, who are quick to arrive.

"Where have you been?" Rausch yells at the security guard. "Do your fucking job."

Rausch turns toward me and it's the first time I see sympathy in his eyes towards me. It's clear he knows who this man is, and a part of me is jealous that my father confided in him and not me, his son.

"You have no right," the man yells while security hauls him away. "I *know* who you are!"

Rausch lets out a deep breath, his eyes narrowed and his lips pursed in anger, but for once, it's not directed at me. I stare after the man I've never known to be my grandfather.

"What the fuck was that?" I ask.

Rausch pinches his forehead as if he's willing a headache to go away. "Not here," he says wearily, and then walks away. I'm unwilling to chase after him, and he's right, this isn't the place.

Up ahead, Alistair and his parents enter the church, and as Evangeline and I walk up the steps to the Cathedral, the press take pictures, shout my name, and one reporter asks who I'm with like this is a fucking movie premier.

"My wife," I growl back in anger, and we walk through the doors of the church. The pews on either side are full of people; people I don't know.

"Darren," Caroline, Alistair's mother, pulls me into a hug and gives me a kiss on the cheek. She pulls away but holds onto me as if checking to make sure I'm still intact.

"I'm so sorry for your loss. Merrill was..." she pauses, choked up, unable to finish.

I look over her shoulder to where Alistair stands, and I can feel the history between our parents that started all the way back at Holy Trinity Preschool.

I take her hand politely – lovingly. "Thank you." I mean it sincerely.

"It's just awful. Isn't it awful Remington?" She turns to her husband, tears in her eyes. Remington hands her a handkerchief, and then holds out a hand to me.

"Anything you need, kid." He gives my hand a manly shake, and I give him a tight nod in return.

Alistair gives me an apologetic smile.

"Did I hear you say wife?" Caroline asks with wide eyes, as if just now remembering, and looks over at Evangeline.

I place a hand at her back. "This is Evangeline."

"Nice to meet you," Evangeline greets, and holds her hand out for Caroline. It takes Caroline a minute to react, unsure of who she is, this newcomer into our inner circle.

"Well," she smiles, and pulls her into a hug, "you're a beautiful girl," I hear her say into Evangeline's hair. "You'll come over for dinner?" She looks at both of us expectantly, and I nod politely, not having any intention of going to their house in the near future.

Still shaken from the altercation outside, I excuse us to head further into the church so we can take our seats.

The minute I step into the nave, I can feel the magnitude of being inside such a building. Even though I am not a God-fearing man, tradition and history are hard to escape. Although the last brick was laid in nineteen-ninety, this church has seen more history than most. the limestone floors have collected the tears, laughter, hushed promises, and desperate prayers of millions of people... and now it will collect mine.

I tilt my head ever so slightly to look at Evangeline, feel her hand in mine once again, and wonder if she feels what I feel... that something old and ancient, not quite spiritual, has taken form.

Church officials direct us to the front of the nave where a pew is reserved for immediate family, and I can't help but notice how empty it is. My mother was an only child, and both of her parents passed years ago. The only family my father had besides me or his estranged brothers was just escorted away from the church.

We slide into the pew, and Evangeline loosens the belt on her jacket, shucking it off and laying it over her lap. She's wearing a black dress with a collar that sits at her neck and a hem that goes almost to her knees.

"Why did you say that?" she whispers.

"Say what?"

"To the press."

I don't get a chance to respond because Rausch and a few of my father's staff slide into the pew next to us. I suppose these people were his family, because he spent more time with them than he did at home with me.

Rausch makes an indignant noise as he fusses with his wool jacket and places it on the pew between himself and Evangeline.

"Did you think I'd turn into ash as soon as I passed through the doors?" I hear her say to him and I stifle a laugh.

"I suppose you and the church have something in common," Rausch retorts as he settles further into his seat. "God welcomes *all*."

Evangeline makes an indignant noise.

All swords are laid down as Mass begins. Halfway through the service, there is a collective noise, like the snap of a rubber band, that echoes throughout the nave when the hassock is pulled out and knees hit the cushion. As the priest reads a prayer from the Old Testament, I look over at Evangeline whose head is bowed, pieces of her blonde hair across her cheeks and her eyes are closed. Although her lips aren't moving, reciting the prayer along with the priest like the rest of the patrons, I can't help but feel as though she's praying too.

My attention is brought back front and center when the priest says *amen*, followed by the sign of the cross, and everyone's voices chime in unison. We sit back onto the bench, and the priest begins reading a eulogy for both my parents. He starts with their participation in the church, generous donations, and unwavering faith, before speaking about their character and accomplishments.

Their lives are summed up, entwined together like carefully tied ribbons that don't reveal their faults, and as the service concludes, the priest reads Psalm 23.

> The LORD is my shepherd;
> I shall not want.
> He maketh me to lie down in green pastures:
> He leadeth me beside the still waters.
> He restoreth my soul.
> *I don't think my soul can be restored.*

I'm supposed to greet people as they leave, say a few words of gratitude to the priest, but I can't bring myself to do it. I meet Evangeline at the end of the pew, grab her hand, and we exit the church.

Behind us is Rausch, his imposing figure taking up more space than necessary.

"Why didn't you want that man here?" I ask without looking behind me.

"Because your father wouldn't have wanted him here," he answers, but I already knew that.

"Is he my grandfather?"

"Spoken like a true lawyer," Rausch chuckles.

"What does that mean?"

"You're asking questions that you already know the answers to."

"Why does everything have to be so difficult with you?" I ask.

"I could say the same about you, Darren."

"Don't make me beg for answers," I say quietly, because that's what he likes to do – lord information over people.

I can hear him sigh behind me. "Go on then."

"What happened between them?" I ask, as the line moves up.

"Despite what you think," Rausch pauses, pulling in a breath, "there are some things even I don't know."

"I find that hard to believe."

Rausch chuckles as if it's an inside joke. "Your father used to say that to me."

I thought it would anger me, being compared to him, but it doesn't.

As soon as we exit the church, Bailey opens the door for us, a solemn look on his face as he nods at me, and I let Evangeline enter first, leaving Rausch to get in the sedan behind us.

We ride in silence the entire way to the National Cemetery as I stare out the window. It's only a twenty-minute drive, and we arrive way too early. Bailey stops the car alongside the gravesite, but I can't bring myself to get out yet.

"I said that you're my wife, because you are." I finally answer her earlier question.

She doesn't say anything; just looks at me as if she's trying to find her way in. I settle back in the leather seat, unbuttoning my suit jacket.

"You might not believe it, but I used to attend Sunday service as a boy. I hated wearing pressed slacks, long-sleeved button-down shirts, and shiny dress shoes, because in summers, it was brutal when the humidity was oppressive. All I wanted to do when I got home was jump straight into the pool, clothes and all. My mother would curse thinking I'd ruin my Sunday clothes in the chlorine, which of course I did, but then there would be another set in my closet the next Sunday to replace them, much to my disappointment."

Evangeline smiles, placing her hand on my thigh.

"My mother would scold me, but then she'd smile and toss my hair as she sent me on my way. She was incredibly forgiving and tolerant, especially with me, because jumping in the pool with my Sunday best on was the least wicked thing I've ever done," I say, smiling at the memory.

"You are far too young to be attending a funeral," she says.

"I could say the same about you." I shrug and then look at the headstones that scatter the hills of the cemetery.

"I'm sure you've heard it a thousand times today, but…"

I know what she's going to say before she says it, because yes, I had heard it a thousand times today, and each time it was like dropping a penny inside a jar, building and building until my anger or resentment was ready to spill over.

"I'm truly sorry for your loss," she says.

I'm not angry because I can tell that she really means it. Our truce is still intact for now.

I nod in return.

"I know you didn't get along with him, but your father," she pauses, seeming to struggle with her words, "he was—well, he seemed to be a very good man."

"Every man's life ends in the same way. It is only the details of how he lived and how he died that distinguish one man from another."

"Hemingway."

I smirk, and she smiles back at me.

16

Grief, Revenge, Spite

Evangeline

I lay awake, staring at the ornamental ceiling. The pattern reminds me of a wedding cake, white and intricate as it spans from the crown molding, and moves inward to the centerpiece, a beautiful chandelier made of brass and crystal. It seems wasted on a guest room, but then every room in the house is decorated just as elaborately. I can't imagine growing up in a place like this, walking on eggshells, afraid to break something.

Rolling over onto my side, I stare at the empty space next to me and hear the patter of rain hit the window. Darren has yet to sleep in this bed with me, not that I expected he would, but he doesn't sleep in any of the other rooms, either. Mostly, I find him asleep on the couch downstairs in the formal living room, with an empty glass of whiskey leaving rings on what I imagine to be an expensive antique table. Tonight though, I hear a piano, the sad notes rising to the second floor.

He never cried.

At the church, during the service, when the priest spoke about Kerry and Merrill, I could hear muffled cries and sniffling, but Darren remained stoic. I would have thought he was an unfeeling statue if it weren't for the tightness of his jaw, like a lock springing into place.

On the chair next to the bed is Darren's Georgetown t-shirt, so I throw it on before padding across the room and down the hall. It's soft and smells like him.

The house is old and drafty, and I've become accustomed to wearing a pair of knee-high socks to keep my feet and legs warm. Darren's t-shirt is big enough to cover the tops of my thighs, but I shiver anyway as I make my way down the stairs.

Next to the piano, flames lick up the sides of the logs in the fireplace, and I can feel the warmth creep up my legs the minute I enter the room. Darren sits on the piano bench, his fingers hovering over the keys, and carelessly sitting on top of the piano is a glass with at least two fingers of whiskey left in it.

He looks so tragically beautiful with his bare feet planted onto the floor, still wearing the white button-down shirt and slacks from the funeral. His brown hair lays in wavy strands, the pieces covering his profile from view.

He starts to play again, a beautiful classical piece. His fingers move over the keys with such familiarity, but he stops in the middle of the song, as if it pains him to continue. Unable to stop myself any longer, I reach for him, first running my fingers through his hair, and he takes a breath, as if my touch has pulled him from whatever murky waters he's drowning in.

A low groan escapes his lips, and he turns around, dragging me on his lap. His hands rest on my hips, and when I look into his eyes, they're a watery green that pull me in until my lips are on his. He tastes like whiskey and grief, and it drags me under, like a hand wrapped around my throat.

I deepen the kiss, while his hands explore underneath my shirt. Goosebumps pebble along my skin, and I push my hands through his thick, wavy hair, just so I can hold on while he stares at me with an intensity that I'm not used to.

It's grief, revenge, spite, and lust, all rolled up into that stare.

"You look good wearing my shirt," he rasps against my skin, while he kisses, sucks, and nips his way along my neck. "But I like it better when it's on the floor." His voice is hoarse, like the crackling of the fire, and I raise my arms so he can pull it over my head. The warmth from the fire feels nice against my bare skin, but it does nothing to stop my nipples from turning into tight points, begging for his mouth and his teeth.

He leans back to look at me, taking in my breasts and my body as if I am something to be worshiped. Running his thumbs over my nipples, he watches as the sensitive skin around them reacts to his touch, turning into an intricate pattern, like a maze. He pulls a nipple into his mouth, his tongue circling, sucking, as he palms each breast, and I squirm on his lap, grinding into him harder, feeling his growing erection against my dampening panties. I close my eyes and tip my head back, holding onto his neck.

He releases my nipple, and I open my eyes to gaze down at him. He looks as if he's drunk, but not from the whiskey. "You're like a drug, Evangeline." he rasps. "I want to bury myself in you until there is nothing left of me."

He moves his hand to the base of my neck, his palm

warm and grounding, pulls me to him, taking my lips in a deep, searching kiss.

I break away from the kiss, pulling on his lower lip as he hisses, and I place my hands on his chest to keep him from pulling me back in. He protests by reaching for me, his eyes searching mine, and I slide off his lap to kneel in front of him.

"You can't look at me like that," he croaks, his voice raw as if he can barely speak.

"Look at you like what?" I smile innocently and sit back on my heels, toes tucked under my backside, as I place my hands on either side of his thighs.

"Like I'm someone to be saved."

I lift his shirt, and he pulls it over his head, throwing it to the side while I unbuckle his belt. The sound of the metal clanking sends a pulse bright and eager at the edges of my womb. I can feel his hardness underneath the expensive material of his pants, and I run my hand up its length, eliciting a groan from Darren who sits patiently watching me.

He likes to watch me.

"Who said anything about saving?" Slowly, I unzip his pants and feel his hands tighten in my hair – desperate, but trying to stay in control. His stomach muscles flutter when I pull out his cock, thick and dark – pre-cum already beading at the top. I look up at him through my lashes and notice his hooded eyes, the hazel now buried deep.

Using my hand, I move up and down his shaft, causing more pre-cum to spill over the top, and I lick my lips, eager to have him in my mouth.

"Jesus Christ, Evangeline," he breathes, a strangled mess. "You're going to make me come without even taking me in your mouth."

Smiling up at him, I use my tongue to lick the tip of his cock, making sure to dig into the slit, causing his thick shaft to jump in response. I take him in my mouth, slowly moving up and down, until I feel Darren's hand in my hair.

"Oh, fuck," he groans, his hand tightening in my hair, pushing and pulling, making me even more wet. I waste no time, sucking hard, taking him deep, and digging my fingers into his thigh.

His pelvis thrusts upwards as if he can't stop himself from fucking my mouth, hitting the back of my throat, and losing himself to me completely.

"Jesus," he pants as he starts to unravel. I want it – I want him to give it to me – but he pulls out before he comes, and I sit back on my heels, wiping my mouth with the back of my hand. Catching his breath, he stares down at me with hooded eyes and grabs my arms, pulling me up and placing me easily onto the piano, the keys making a discordant sound as my feet slide across them.

"You're too good at that," he says while his fingers grip my waist.

"At least you're getting your money's worth," I remind him.

He smiles, gripping my panties on either side, causing me to lift my hips so he can pull them off.

"Open your thighs for me, Queenie," he says, and I do. I didn't like the use of the nickname before, but tonight, while he's sitting in front of me at eye level with my pussy, I shiver in response. The cool air hits my bare, wet cunt, and I shiver again. Running a finger up my center, he hums as if he's pleased with how wet I am, and I squirm for more.

"Did sucking my cock make you wet?" he asks in a deep, seductive voice.

"Yes," I answer honestly while I spread my legs further apart to give him more access. He parts my lips with his thumbs and licks up the center, making me squirm for more.

"Do you know how fucking sweet you taste?"

The sight of his dark head between my thighs threatens to unravel me, a tremor starting in my stomach, and the more he sucks and licks, the more my thighs shake. It doesn't take much to push me towards the edge, because I was already wet and throbbing with his cock in my mouth.

My moans seem to echo, like the piano, musical and haunting.

"Are you going to come for me?" he asks, kissing the bare spot above my clit while he pushes a finger inside me, hooking just right to press against my wall. My palms push against the smooth surface of the piano, and I can only moan my response while he pumps his fingers inside me, sucking and nipping his way over my thighs and my cunt. My stomach shakes every time his tongue runs over my clit, keeping my orgasm at bay.

"Darren," I whimper for more.

"You only come for me," he demands, setting the gears of my climax in motion. "I want you to come – just for me," he orders in a breathless tone, and I'm a ticking time bomb just waiting to explode. "Can you do that – can you do that for me?" His desperate plea tugs at the edges of my womb like the catch of a wick.

"Yes," I breathe heavily, grabbing his hair and pulling him closer, holding him in place as he explores my pussy with his fingers and his mouth, burning brighter and hotter, moving along my spine, and causing every muscle in my body to twitch. I come for him, shuddering and shaking. I tip my head back and lean into it as it rips through me.

His fingers remain inside me, pressing against my front wall while I start to come down from the high, and my vision clears, the room coming back into focus. I lean down to kiss him, tasting myself on his tongue. He lifts me off the piano and I wrap my arms around his neck lazily, my body limp. We stare at each other for a heartbeat and he kisses me – the slow and steady kind that makes you weak in the knees before he sets me down on the rug in front of the fire.

He rips open a condom and slides it on, his thighs pushing mine apart, my knees settled against his ribcage. He grabs hold of his shaft and lines it up to my entrance, the tip grazing against my still-sensitive clit. He pushes in quickly, fucking me hard, to the cadence of the pounding rain against the window, his name escaping my lips and being captured by the bricks of the fireplace, in the paint strokes of the artwork, and the ivory keys of the piano, transforming this room from hollow… to something that resembles life.

17
Get Your Own

Evangeline

I lean over the kitchen island and dip my chopsticks into Darren's kung pao chicken. He bats me away playfully, but not before I'm able to abscond with a piece of his chicken.

"You have your own," he scolds. His hair falls into his face, teasing the tops of his brows.

The early morning light filters through the window, and somehow, eating leftover Chinese food for breakfast tastes better than it did when it was delivered hot and fresh last night.

"But yours is better," I reply before plopping the piece of chicken in my mouth.

"What's wrong with yours?" he asks, poking at my container with his chopstick.

"It's not spicy," I say, making a sad face while looking inside my carton.

"Why didn't you order something spicy?" he asks, putting a protective arm around his meal.

"Because then I wouldn't be able to steal yours." I try to grab another piece of his chicken, following him around the counter.

"Get your own," he teases and bats me away again, moving to the other side of the island to put distance between us, a boyish smirk tugging at his lips. It feels like we're just two careless young adults enjoying a meal without any of the loss or disappointment of life.

This kitchen has been a neutral space, where we can just be ourselves, and Darren lets his guard down. It reminds me of the kitchen in the house I grew up in, when my grandfather was alive, and my grandmother was well. It's not as grand as this kitchen, but it still has the ability to pull truths in a way no other room can, no matter its size or the quality of the craftsmanship.

The room becomes quiet and somber as Darren peers across the island, a rare look of remorse on his face. "I'm sorry," he whispers, barely audible, but it sits heavy on his lips, and my heart stops for a beat because I wasn't expecting that.

I don't want to hear it – I don't want to be reminded of how this started, or think about where it's going, because it causes the guilt to sit low and heavy inside me. His 'sorry' drifts over the cartons scattered on top of the island, and I pretend not to hear it as I push them out of the way, using one of the bar stools to climb up onto the island. Darren watches with a curious eye as I stalk towards him on all fours like a predator, my knee-high socks making it easy to slide along the marble.

He swallows hard, the apology forgotten, replaced by the tug of desire. When I reach him, I sit back on my heels and smile, my eyes dropping to the container in his hand.

"Do you want a piece of my chicken?" he asks with a wicked smile on his handsome face.

He's the careless kind of handsome, with long black lashes that women would kill for – the wicked kind of handsome that makes you forget what a pretentious asshole he is.

I sit on the island like a dog begging for a treat. "Yes," I answer.

He dips his chopsticks into the carton, but before he pulls out a piece of chicken, he raises his eyes back up to me. "Take your shirt off."

Without hesitation, I grab the hem of my shirt and pull it over my head, shaking out my hair. His eyes drop to my bare breasts.

"Mm. No bra," he groans. "Good girl."

I lean forward, my breasts hanging between us and open my mouth, waiting for my prize. He places the piece of chicken on my tongue, and I grab the carton, jumping off the counter, and racing out of the kitchen.

"Evangeline!" Darren bellows.

When I get to the beginning of the long hallway, I can hear his bare feet against the wood flooring behind me.

"You better run," he calls, and I giggle in response, "because if I catch you…" he pauses, and I wait with bated breath for him to finish, to tell me what he will do if he catches me. "You *will* regret it." I can hear him grit his teeth and feel his fingers brush my hip while I turn into one of the rooms.

I squeal with laughter, holding onto the contents of the container while he spins me around, and I toss a few pieces of chicken at his bare chest.

He lets go, looking down at the sauce and noodles that stick to his skin.

"You're gonna pay for that." He grabs onto my ass, lifting me up and turning me around.

He crashes his hungry mouth to mine. I stop struggling against him and lean into his kiss, feeling his hands knead both my cheeks. "Jesus, this ass, it's fucking perfect," he groans, palming me.

"Does that mean I'm forgiven?" I smile against his lips and wrap my legs around his waist.

He pulls his mouth from mine. "You play dirty," he groans, looking down at the sticky sauce that clings to both my breasts, and he licks his lips. "I like it." A pulse runs down my stomach and right to my pussy at just the thought of him licking the sauce from my body.

Setting me down on my feet, his eyes drop to my breasts. "What are you going to do about it?" I ask, looking up at him through my lashes.

He swallows hard and then he grabs me by the waist, holding me tight to him. I blow out a breath, anticipating his mouth on me.

His hands move up my body and my breath hitches, but instead of taking me into his mouth, he starts to tickle me.

I laugh, shocked and embarrassed that he tricked me. "You're an asshole!" I yell between fits of laughter as I struggle against him.

"So I've heard," he bites out, laughing so hard he can barely hold onto me anymore.

I take the opportunity to squirm out of his hold.

I run back down the hall towards the kitchen, leaving the partially empty carton on the floor. When I get to the end of the hall and turn to enter the kitchen, a woman is standing by the island. Darren crashes into me.

"Lottie!" he yells, and casually walks over, giving her a hug and lifting her feet slightly off the ground.

"Darren!" she scolds him loudly. "You put me down!" She smacks his arm and Darren sets her feet back on the ground. She smiles at him while touching his face in a motherly kind of way.

"Darren," she says his name again softly, and the moment becomes heavy, the laughter squeezed out of the room. "I'm so sorry." Her eyes look as though tears will spill over any minute. Darren smiles at her in a way I've never seen him smile at anyone. Not even the laugh I elicited from him earlier rivals this smile. A pebble of jealousy starts to grow in my belly but I quickly push it down when Darren turns proudly, his arm around the woman. "Lottie, this is my wife, Evangeline."

I quickly cross my arms over my chest, embarrassed.

"Your wife?" Lottie asks, shocked.

"Yeah, it kinda happened fast," Darren says, rubbing the back of his neck and raising his eyebrows at me. "I'm so glad you're back." He gives her another hug.

"I'm gonna go and get dressed," I say, hooking my thumb in the direction of the stairs.

"It was nice meeting you," Lottie says politely.

I nod and exit the kitchen. As I leave, I hear Lottie say, "She's beautiful, Darren."

He replies, "Yeah, she is."

"Tell me everything," I hear Lottie say, but I don't hear his response. I wonder exactly what he will tell her. Maybe he should explain that he fucked me out of my contract at the agency and coerced me into marrying him so he could get his family's money.

"Evangeline?"

I turn around, looking over Darren's shoulder to see that he's alone.

"I'm sorry about that." He tips his head in the direction of the kitchen. "I forgot she was coming by today." He shakes his head in apology.

"It's fine," I say, pushing a few stray pieces of hair from my face. "This is your house."

He pinches his eyebrows at my choice of words. His arm rests on the post of the stairs while I stand on the first step, making us equal in height.

"I know," he says, gripping the post. "I, uh," he pauses, shaking his head as if to unstick the words in his throat. "Just wanted to make sure you were okay."

"I'm fine." I realize that I'm being irrational and cold, but I just want to go upstairs and dress.

Darren nods, his hand moving from the post, and I go up the stairs to the guest room I've been occupying. I sit for a minute, looking around the room – my clothes are strewn over furniture and occupying parts of the floor. I wasn't like this in my apartment. I was clean and organized, but somehow, being here has turned me into someone who leaves their clothes all over the place, throws food in the kitchen, and leaves leftovers spilled in the hallway. What must Lottie think of me?

I reach into my bag for my phone. I haven't bothered to turn it on since I got here. It vibrates in my hand and I look down at the screen. There are a few messages from Cleo, and one from a number I don't recognize, but I know the message is from my mother.

18
You Don't Marry Them

Darren

Reality never sets in harder than when Rausch is in front of me. I can tell he doesn't like that I'm sitting behind my father's desk while he's on the other side.

"Do you have no sense?" he starts off by saying. "You told the press you're married?" he continues.

"I didn't hold a press conference."

"Everything's a joke to you. You told a reporter she," he gestures somewhere in the house, "is your wife."

"She is." I settle into the leather high-back chair, turning a pen between my fingers.

"You don't tell the fucking *press* that."

I shrug. "What does it matter?"

"Have you picked up a paper lately?" he asks, and then gestures towards the front of the house. "Or looked out your front door?"

"I've been busy." I give him a suggestively arched brow.

He curls his lip in response and stands abruptly.

I follow him reluctantly because he looks like he has a point to make. When we reach the formal living room, he opens the curtain slightly to reveal a few reporters waiting on the sidewalk in front of the gate.

In all the years my father was a Senator, there have never been reporters on our front lawn.

"What the fuck?"

"Yeah. What the fuck, Darren?" Rausch parrots.

Telling *one* reporter that Evangeline was my wife wouldn't garner this much attention, would it?

"What do they want?" I ask.

"They want to know why the late Senator Walker's *only son* got married not a day after he *fucking died*!"

"How would they know *when* I got married?"

"Marriage licenses are public record!"

I didn't think of that. I look past Rausch to see a few reporters loitering on the street as if they have nothing better to do.

"*The Post* deems this news?" This doesn't seem like news to me, but what reporters deem as *news* is beyond me these days.

"I'm pretty sure Broadsheets have better things to do. These are reporters from the popular press – *tabloids*," he says with distaste.

When I look at him with confusion, he sighs. "The tabloids pick this up and it gets attention, *The* fucking *Post* might as well report it!"

"I don't give a fuck what they think." I throw my hands in the air. "They can stand out there all they fucking want because I don't owe them anything."

"It's only a matter of time before they find out she's a prostitute, Darren," he continues. Rausch moves closer, looming over me. "You *fuck* prostitutes, Darren. You don't *marry* them."

I storm out of the living room and back down the hall towards the office, but Rausch stops me.

"This," he points towards the front door, "is not something you can run or hide from forever, Darren. Whether you like it or not, your parents were prominent figures in Washington. Your mother served on many charity boards that still need to be handled." He walks into my father's office and stretches his arms out. "You wanted to run the estate? Well, this is running it. Grow the fuck up!"

I knew Rausch was so tangled up in my parents' business that it would be hard to cut him from the brambles, but I never thought of a scenario where I would be willing to wait to cut him free. I need him right now, and he knows it.

"Their staff can handle all of this," I say, punting responsibility elsewhere because I don't want it.

"You really don't understand how things work," Rausch growls and leans so far over the desk that I can smell his breath. He might be right about that, but I wasn't going to let him know that.

"I don't care how it used to work," I retort and shake my head.

"Your mother raised money for domestic violence victims. She created the Abigail Pershing Foundation, which provides safe houses for women." Rausch steps back from the desk and turns to look at the bookshelf while he rubs his neck. "Are you going to let them down?" His voice changes, becoming lower, more cautious, and full of emotion.

I can't see his face, but I know he can feel my father in this room just as much as I do. He's everywhere; in the spines of each book, molded into the carvings in the corners of the wood door frames, and reflected back at me in the windowpane that looks out to the side yard. It occurs to me how much Rausch has been a part of my parents' lives, even before my father ran for office.

"Were you in love with my mother?"

"Why would you ask me such a question?" His blue eyes flare with anger.

"Were you?" I press further.

He takes a moment before answering as if choosing his words carefully.

"I loved *both* of your parents," he says with conviction and rare emotion. "I don't want to see their legacies die with them."

I don't know whether I believe him or not, but he is right about one thing, at least; I don't want my mother to be forgotten. Rausch might be an asshole, but he'd never steered my father wrong, and he was always there for my mother.

"You can hate your father all you want, Darren, but you can never escape being his son."

His words land like a heavy crown placed upon my head, the weight almost crippling. The responsibility is something I've been running from my whole life. "I didn't ask to be his son."

"But you are, and the sooner you accept it, the easier it will be."

The mention of fathers and sons reminds me of something. "I will take responsibility for my mother's charity."

Rausch gives me an approving nod.

"But in return, you will tell me about my grandfather."

Wet leaves cling to the grass, even as the sun shines through a few stubborn clouds. I used to like fall, the way the leaves changed colors, a signal of the impending holiday seasons. Evangeline hands me a jacket as she sits down on the bench next to me. She doesn't say anything, just watches the birds in the tree. She's very good at knowing when to sit in the silence, and when not to.

"Halloween was my favorite holiday as a kid," I say without looking at her. "It was the one holiday that was *actually* fun." I smile at the memory of our street transforming with decorations and groups walking house to house. "It was the one time when the other kids were excited to visit our house, not because of who my father was, but because he wore the best Dracula costume and scared the crap out of everyone," I laugh.

"I can't even imagine," she laughs, pressing a fist to her mouth.

"Yeah, well, this was before he became too serious."

I push my arms through the sleeves of the jacket, pulling it tight around my body against the chilly air. "Thanksgiving and Christmas were full of obligations, and stuffy parties I was invited to so my parents could show off how well I played the piano," I continue.

"You do play beautifully," she says, the pink in her cheeks darkening.

I nod, looking down at the wet stones surrounding the bench. "I wanted to make my mother happy. The better I got, the more attention I got." I laugh. "It's stupid, I know," I say.

"I think it's normal that every kid wants to make their

parents proud," she says, placing a comforting hand on my thigh, and I can feel the misery in her touch. It seeps through my jeans and right into my thigh, burrowing itself deep into my bones. Like calls to like, and I have no doubt she understands, but I'm too fucking selfish to ask her about it, not that I think she'd tell me anyway. I'd rather be alone in my misery right now.

Instead, I snort. "Well, I wasn't very good at making my parents proud," I say, shifting my position on the bench to face her. "Fuckup after fuckup."

"So they didn't expect anything else," she confirms, hitting the nail on the head so cleanly that I don't even feel it pierce my skin.

"Do your parents know what you do?"

"No," she says looking up at the leaves that seem to be holding in the sunlight that breaks through the clouds, "they're dead."

I don't ask her to elaborate because I don't think she'd tell me the truth anyway, so I let it go.

She crosses her legs and shifts towards me. "Are the reporters outside of the house because of me?" she asks, changing the subject.

I sit up straighter and sigh. "They're here because of me."

"I heard what Rausch said. I wasn't trying to eavesdrop," she's quick to add, "but he can be loud."

"Are you worried about it?"

She lets out a breath. "Darren, I know what and who I am. I'm not worried about me," she pauses. "I'm worried about you."

"Fuck." I run a hand through my hair. "I don't deserve that."

"You don't," she says, resolutely, "but I'm feeling

generous today, so don't piss me off and make me take it back because I'll open the front door and throw you to the wolves."

I raise my arm and place it over the back of the bench. "I'd prefer being thrown to the wolves than attending a charity event," I say, raising an eyebrow.

"Charity event?"

I give her a wolfish grin. "Do you like masquerade balls?"

19

Squirrel

Evangeline

I'm about to step into the kitchen but stop abruptly, noticing Lottie at the sink drying dishes. At least I have clothes on this time.

She gives me a warm smile. "Can I get you anything?"

"No, I was just going to grab a cup of coffee."

Lottie grabs the cup before I'm able to. "No, no, honey, let me get it for you."

I concede by taking a seat at the island while she operates the espresso machine with familiarity. "I'm sorry about the other day," I tell her. I want to say that I don't normally run through a house naked, but that'd be a lie. She places the cup of coffee in front of me and I smile, looking down at my hands as I wrap them around the cup. "I just didn't want you to think…"

"Mrs. Walker," she says, and I look up, eyes wide.

"Please," I reply, "Evangeline."

Lottie nods. "Evangeline," her brown eyes take on a knowing gleam. "You have nothing to worry about."

I get the feeling that my bare breasts are probably the least of the questionable things she's seen over the years. "You've worked here a long time, haven't you?"

"Ever since Darren was a little boy." Lottie says with pride. "Would you like a scone?" She pushes the plate piled high with flaky pastries closer to me. They're still so hot I can see the steam rising off them, but I shake my head, not having much of an appetite.

"I make a really great omelet too," she offers, wiping her hands on a towel and then placing it on her shoulder.

"Coffee's fine," I say, holding up the cup and taking a sip.

She tilts her head. "You're uncomfortable."

I laugh nervously, setting the cup back down. "No, you're fine."

"I meant, you're uncomfortable being taken care of," she corrects, like she can see through me to all of my disappointments. Lottie seems like the kind of woman who is observant enough to notice, but smart enough not to call attention to it. That's how she's outlasted everyone here – everyone except Darren.

"I didn't grow up like this," I admit and motion around the chef's kitchen.

"I didn't either, if it makes you feel better." Lottie smiles wide, accentuating the crow's feet on either side of her soft brown eyes. She looks to be in her fifties—not old, but not young either. Her hands are telling – large knuckles and swollen fingers – that she's spent most of her life taking care of other people. If she's worked for the Walker family since Darren was little, then she must have started really young.

"I hope you don't mind that Darren is having me come twice a week to take care of some of the household duties," she says. "If there's anything you need from the grocery store besides the usual, just add it to the list." She points to the notepad clipped to the refrigerator.

"I'm afraid that's my fault."

Lottie tilts her head in question.

"The press are here because of me."

"The press are like dogs," she explains. "Another squirrel will get their attention, and they'll be in the neighbor's yard before you know it."

I can't help but laugh. "That's an optimistic way of looking at it."

"Only way to get through it," she says. "Until then and even beyond, if you have any preferences on groceries, just let me know."

"Oh, whatever Darren wants," I say, waving her off.

"Honey, this is your house now, too," Lottie says while wiping down the counter. That may be temporarily true, but it doesn't feel like it.

I take in a deep breath, the smell of the cooling scones still permeating the air. "I don't know what Darren told you…"

"He told me that you saved him."

I wonder if that's what Darren really said, or if that's what she so kindly inferred from whatever story he told her, but either way, it's not true. Her expression turns serious, and she places a hand over mine in a kind gesture, warm and motherly. "After what happened to his parents, I thought he would be alone." She looks at me with a thoughtful expression. "Until you."

I open my mouth to correct her, although I have no idea what to say, but then Darren enters the kitchen and Lottie pulls her hand away.

"Don't believe anything Lottie tells you," Darren greets

as he enters the kitchen and grabs a scone from the plate in the middle of the island, making a pleased sound as he takes a bite.

"So you *didn't* pee your bed when you were ten?" I ask, narrowing my eyes at him.

"What? No!" He looks horrified.

Lottie laughs while Darren's eyes light up. "I think you may have met your match, Darren."

Darren takes another bite of his scone. "You have no idea," he grumbles, chewing the pastry.

I take a sip of my coffee with satisfaction.

20
Dog and Pony Show

Evangeline

"I thought you were joking that it was a masquerade ball," I say, while Darren holds the mask in his hand.

"Unfortunately, no."

He turns me around to face the mirror while he brings the mask over my eyes and ties it at the back. It's made of red silk and glitter, covering the upper half of my face with an intricate design that wraps around the sides and top.

The dress is made of a thin red silk that hugs every curve. The slit up the side goes all the way to the very top of my thigh.

"Really, Darren?" I roll my eyes at him as I look at myself in the mirror.

He leans close to my ear. "This is for the shirts – and the underwear."

I narrow my eyes at him.

He gives me a devilish smile while gathering my hair

in his fist, holding it away from my face, and causing goosebumps along my back. "I think your hair would look lovely held back. Shows off your beautiful neck," he murmurs.

"I thought this was for a charity, not a burlesque show?" I clear my throat and smooth down the dress as he backs away from me.

"That's appropriate, because charity events are a sort of dog and pony show." He lifts an eyebrow. "Besides, the cost per plate plus the money raised at the silent auction all go to the domestic violence charity my mother supported," Darren explains.

"How much does each plate cost?" I ask, gathering my hair and twisting it into a low bun.

Darren gives me one of his wolfish smiles as he adjusts his bowtie in the mirror behind me. "You don't want to know," he says, and perhaps he's right.

For someone who claims to hate these types of events, he sure has made an attempt to look nothing less than striking in his black tux that shows off his broad shoulders and lean waist. For once, he's managed to wrangle each strand of dark hair to stay in place. He almost – *almost* – looks respectable, if it wasn't for the perpetual glint of mischief in his eyes.

He takes hold of my hand, turning me around to face him. His eyes drop to my lips, as if he's debating whether it's worth it to smear my red lipstick. I take in a shaky breath and feel the air fill up my chest as his lips hover over mine.

The decision was made when he releases me, and it's like the world snaps back into place.

"We should get going," he says, holding out his arm for

me to take. I slip the mask off for the ride over and tuck it into my small purse.

It's been a week since the press have been camped outside of the house, and just like Lottie said, a new squirrel caught their attention – but that doesn't mean they've forgotten. Darren advised that Rausch had taken measures to minimize the press presence, and I don't want to know what it takes to suppress free speech, but I'm glad they've left the front of the house.

While I've been to dinners and fancy events before, never have I gone as someone's *wife*. Staring out the window, I watch as the city goes by, little twinkling lights enveloped in a blanket of midnight blue.

I notice Darren nervously checks the inside of his jacket pocket again where he stuffed his notecards.

"You went to law school," I muse. "I thought speaking in front of a room full of people was like second nature?"

"Contrary to popular belief, I'm not good at everything."

"Then what are you good at?"

Darren turns to me, his lips tugging into a wicked smile. "You, of all people, shouldn't have to ask."

I narrow my eyes at him, but inside, my stomach twists into knots because yes, there is something Darren is *very* good at.

"I doubt the patrons of the charity event will give you credit for your excellence at eating pussy," I say, clasping my hands demurely in my lap.

Darren chuckles, leaning in close to my ear. "Be careful, Evangeline, or I will show you what else I'm good at – and it has nothing to do with that sweet cunt of yours."

I swallow hard, turning my head to look out the window again, but I can't help squirming in my seat.

"So why are you giving a speech if you don't like it?" I ask.

Darren rubs his forehead. "It's too late to back out now," he says. "The foundation thought it would be beneficial to have someone from the *Walker* family give a speech."

"Maybe get a few more donations."

Darren purses his lips into a flat smile. "Now you're thinking like a true D.C. socialite."

"I don't take that as a compliment."

"It wasn't meant to be."

"Why domestic violence?" I've wanted to ask ever since I found out about his mother's involvement in the foundation, but there never seemed to be a quiet moment to do so.

Darren chuckles. "She wasn't a victim, if that's what you're asking."

"No, I just want to know more about her." Darren seemed so fond of her, and selfishly, I wanted to know what her life was like with Kerry – things you couldn't find out on the internet.

"My mother was a proud debutante," he says, smiling as if he's conjuring a memory. "She comes from a long line of politicians, and she knows—*knew*—what it meant," he corrects himself, "to have lived a life of service."

"She picked domestic violence as her cause because of an incident that happened at my father's campaign headquarters." His ominous tone doesn't leave room for me to inquire more on the subject.

"How did she meet your father?" I dare to ask.

Darren stretches his long legs out in front of him, crossing one ankle over the other casually.

"My father grew up in rural Virginia. He came from

nothing, but managed to get some scholarships to attend college. He met my mother at Georgetown, and," he pauses, smiling, "well, the rest is history."

"What kind of story is that, coming from a man who can quote Emerson on a whim?" I chide him.

Darren laughs softly. "I'm sorry my storytelling abilities aren't up to your standards,"

"I feel sorry for the guests at the dinner," I tease.

His expression grows melancholy. "She told me that she never saw anyone study so hard. My dad was the last one to leave the library every night. She thought he was so driven because he was trying to outrun his meager beginnings. All the boys in her circle never had to work hard for anything," he says with a little reluctance. "She admired him for that."

I listen intently, selfishly lapping up every private detail of Kerry's story.

He seems to snap out of the memory and turns to me. "When my dad was campaigning, she organized the volunteers and met an eager young woman who wanted to work the phones. Her name was Abigail Pershing."

"That's the name of the foundation," I say softly.

"She didn't like talking about it, and I didn't ask," Darren admits.

The car pulls up to the curb, stunting the conversation. "You didn't say it was at The Smithsonian," I state, seeing the partial lettering on the outside of the building. I know that I sound intimidated, but I can't help it.

"The National Portrait Museum," he corrects, and before I can say anything else, Bailey opens the door, holding out his hand for me.

Behind us is a line of cars with their doors open, the patrons exiting towards the wide set of stone stairs leading up to the museum's columned entrance. The Greek revival architecture with its white and stately elegance looks as though it takes up the entire city block.

A sea of people dressed in decadent colors, windswept skirts, and flapping overcoats, climb the stairs towards the entrance. Before we get to the stairs, Darren motions for me to put on my mask as he secures his own, made of black velvet and lined with silver sequins.

I notice a small crowd of press gathering near the entrance.

"The advantage of it being a masquerade ball," Darren winks, although I'd know his hazel eyes anywhere.

The event is held in the Kogod Courtyard, a large open space that looks as if you're standing on a city street. Down the middle atop black granite flooring are large, round tables draped with beautiful linens, a display of flowers, and lit candles in the center of each. A combination of up lighting and flickering candles give the space a magical feel, but nothing compares to the canopy of the wavy glass and steel structure that appears to float over the courtyard, keeping out the elements.

I can see right through the ceiling to the cloudless, inky sky that holds billions and billions of stars, but only a handful are visible tonight.

All of the women are wearing beautiful gowns, dripping in diamonds, and even though we're all wearing masks, it's hard not to notice certain members of Washington's elite, some of whom have been clients.

Jonathan could be here.

I've never felt more out of place in my Jessica Rabbit style dress, and I could strangle Darren right now for picking it out.

I touch my mask, making sure it's still in place, using it to hide my identity in more ways than one.

Darren, sensing my trepidation, grabs my attention, pointing to an older, distinguished-looking man with a much younger woman.

"Donald Archer. He owns a media strategy company. Just celebrated his sixty-eighth birthday last month," Darren says, raising an eyebrow, and I can see the mischief in his eyes as he continues. "And his wife, Hillary Crist-Archer, who gave up a thriving career as a hostess at Marcel's near Capitol Hill to marry the love of her life," Darren says, sarcastically.

"Darren Walker, you're an incorrigible gossip," I joke with him, shaking my head.

"Is that a good thing?" he asks, leaning in close to hear my answer, and I can feel his smile against my cheek.

"Depends," I tease as we walk around the room and attract a few curious stares. My mask doesn't seem to be hiding as much as I'd hoped, but I doubt they're looking at my face.

"Depends on what?" he asks.

"What other gossip do you have?" I squeeze his arm, and he points me in the direction of a stately older woman with beautiful silver hair. Her dress is very stylish and elegant, with a white top that looks like a blouse, but the skirt is a royal blue and flared at the waist, and it seems to reflect the lighting in the courtyard.

"That's Bethany York. She's retiring from the National Archives Museum, but it seems she's taken on a new job," Darren says cryptically, not hiding his excitement in the least.

"Don't tell me," I say, tapping my finger to my chin, "she's a dominatrix at an underground sex club."

He shrugs and my mouth drops open. "Alistair swears by it," Darren says, giving me his wolfish grin, and all of the nervous energy from earlier vanishing.

I look at him incredulously. "Well, Alistair is a reliable source." I roll my eyes.

Darren steers me towards the silent auction when someone collides into him from the small alcove at the back of the table. Even though he's wearing a mask, I can tell it's Alistair.

"Dare," Alistair says in surprise, greeting him with a smack on his arm.

The fly of his trousers is partially down. I cough loudly, getting his attention and lowering my eyes. Alistair follows my gaze and as discreetly as he can, zips.

"You look lovely," he says, admiring my dress.

I narrow my eyes at him but then widen them when Hillary Crist-Archer appears from the shadows of the alcove, smoothing down her dress. One of the jeweled pins in her hair has come undone. She ignores Alistair, of course, and rushes by, getting swallowed up in the crowd.

Darren coughs, pressing his fist into his mouth, trying to hide his laughter.

"What?" Alistair asks, holding his hands up while Darren shakes his head.

An older woman who looks to be in her fifties, dressed in a beautiful robin's egg blue gown walks in our direction.

"Another dominatrix?" I whisper to Darren jokingly.

"Something like that," he whispers back, and then plasters on a charming smile. "She's very good at whipping donations out of people."

"Darren, I've been looking for you," the woman says with a wide smile.

"These masks aren't doing their job," he jokes, and rips it off in order to give her a peck on the cheek.

"Alistair," she looks in his direction, saying his name tightly as if she's already aware of his reputation.

"Audrina," Alistair takes her hand and dramatically makes a show of kissing the top of it.

"Can we count on you for a generous donation?" she asks.

"My parents wrote a check earlier."

"Just your parents?"

"Does it count if they put my name on it?"

She narrows her eyes at him. "No."

Pulling her hand back, she turns her attention to Darren. "Some of the other committee members would like to meet you," she says, and then notices me standing next to him. "My apologies," she says, then looks at Darren to introduce us.

"Audrina Ellwood, this is my wife, Evangeline," he says to my surprise, and then rests his palm against the small of my back. "Audrina's the one that coerced me into making a speech," he teases.

She laughs. "Coerced is such a strong word," she replies, raising a teasing eyebrow at Darren.

"Nice to meet you," I respond politely and take her hand in mine.

"Ah yes, I heard you got married," Audrina says coyly. News spreads like foraging wasps in this group. "She's very beautiful," Audrina says to Darren as if he purchased a show horse. "You must tell me how you met," she asks expectantly.

Darren and I never discussed what we'd say if people asked, and I gaze at him with my mouth open, trying to think of something plausible.

"Oh, well, I paid her five million dollars to marry me," he says straight-faced.

If I'd had something to drink, I would have spit it out all over Audrina's expensive dress.

"How else do you think I would get someone as exquisite as her to marry me?" he asks with a wink.

Audrina lets out a laugh.

Alistair coughs into his fist and then adjusts his bowtie once more while he stands awkwardly at Darren's side.

"Darren," she exclaims, swatting his arm playfully, "you really do take after your father; so charming and quick-witted." Audrina continues to laugh lightly, and even though Darren's smiling, I can feel the muscles in his arms tense at being compared to his father.

"You have your work cut out with this one," Audrina declares as she addresses me.

"I already know all about that," I reply while giving her a tight smile.

"Do you mind if I steal him away?" Audrina asks.

"Just bring him back without any marks," I tease while Darren makes a choking noise.

"Not any that you could see, dear," Audrina teases back, but I find her straight face arresting as she waits politely.

"I won't be long," Darren assures me. "Dare I say Alistair will keep you company?" He raises a questioning eyebrow at Alistair.

"That's fine, I need an alibi anyway." He winks at me while Darren gives him a stern look.

Before he's whisked away, he leans into me and whispers, "Don't get lost, Queenie," he says in a voice as deep as midnight. "I have something to show you later."

But then he's gone, disappearing into a sea of black and

white tuxedos as I wonder what he's up to while I'm left with Alistair.

"I would attempt to make an excuse for what you witnessed earlier, but I don't think you care," he says apathetically. "Shall we?" He motions towards the bar across the room, draped with a red tablecloth and adorned with different kinds of liquor bottles.

"Yes, please." I follow his lead, making my way through the crowd, and noticing masks laying discarded on tables and used as placeholders on chairs. When we get to the bar, Alistair orders a jack and coke on the rocks with a lime, and then he gestures towards me.

"Champagne," I say to the bartender.

While waiting, I pull my phone out of my purse to check the time when I see another message from my mother. I never answered her text the other day, and I don't plan on responding now. I have a feeling it's because she may have seen an article about Darren and I getting married, even all the way in Arizona.

With a sour face, I slide the phone back in my purse.

"Already checking to see how much longer you'll have to stay?" Alistair asks, taking our drinks from the bartender and handing me the champagne flute as we move to the side.

"You don't have to babysit me."

He chuckles. "As long as we've got that out of the way," he states, taking a sip of his drink. "You look like the kind of girl who can take care of herself, but this is a room full of sharks in tuxedos and ball gowns."

"I was thinking wolves," I quip, turning towards him.

"Wolves are too gentle," he pauses and wags his finger before adding, "They actually take care of their young,"

Alistair finishes and raises an eyebrow, causing me to scoff.

He takes another drink of his jack and coke before continuing. "Now sharks, they give birth and leave their young to fend for themselves."

"Did you learn that at Georgetown?" I ask, taking a sip of my champagne.

"They don't teach life lessons at Georgetown," he replies deadpan and raises his eyebrows at me.

If this is supposed to make me feel sorry for him or even Darren, it doesn't, but he doesn't give me a chance to respond. He tips his empty glass in my direction. "Stay out of trouble, Evangeline." With a wink, he heads in the direction of where Darren is having an animated conversation with a group of guests.

Alistair is getting inside my head, because I think about how Darren harbors deep resentment towards his father, and I'm trying to make sense of it. I know I shouldn't be thinking about this – not tonight – not ever again, but the Kerry Walker *I knew* – well, he wasn't *my* father – far from it. He was just a man who loved Emerson, and in turn, inspired a love of Emerson in me.

The group laughs at something Darren says, pulling my attention back to them, and a woman with auburn hair and an emerald-green A-line dress touches his arm. This is a different side of him that I've never seen; charming and warm, albeit the slightest bit tight. He grew up in this life, whether he rejected it or not, and he's still one of them… and it is all the more apparent that I am not. I take a sip of my champagne when I feel someone stand beside me.

"And to think he's only scratching the surface of his potential," Rausch says close to my ear. His cologne smells like deep woods and dark caves.

He's turning a glass tumbler of something amber around in his hand as he watches Darren with a satisfied smile on his face, almost as if he's a proud parent.

He looks very different in black tie – almost handsome. I begin to wonder if Rausch is a wolf or a shark.

Frustrated, I pull the mask from my face. "I suppose these do little to provide anonymity," I say with frustration while tucking it into my purse.

Rausch makes a throaty noise. "I don't need to see your face to know it's you."

Ignoring his comment, I turn back towards the crowd to avoid letting him know that he's getting to me. Rausch is a hard read. Because of that, just his presence in the room makes me uncomfortable.

"Did Darren pick this out?" he asks, pointing to my dress.

I glare at him with a look that says, *do you think I would pick this out on my own?*

Rausch laughs. "Well, he always did like flaunting his trophies." He shoves a hand in his pocket and surveys the room.

"He looks like he's raising a lot of money for the foundation." I move around the edge of the room towards the table displaying the silent auction. "Isn't that what you wanted?" I muse.

"Among other things."

I look at the cards on the table, displaying items such as plastic surgery with a top-notch L.A. surgeon, a private tour of the museum, lunch with a famous actor, a vacation rental in Aspen, a trip to Paris, the items seem endless.

"Jesus," I whisper.

"All the wealth in this room must be good for something," Rausch challenges.

"We both know why you're talking to me, and it's not because you find my company enthralling."

"Ah well, you're wrong. I do find your company enthralling, Ms. Bowen."

"Mrs. Walker," I correct him.

I feel him bristle next to me. He lets out a long sigh. "Darren's a child, he still thinks with his cock."

"Don't all men?"

Rausch shrugs. "True *men* know when not to listen."

"I just want my money and to move on, not to be some chess piece between you and Darren." I narrow my eyes at him.

"You married into the wrong family for that, I'm afraid."

There's an announcement at the podium and everyone turns their attention to the front of the atrium where Audrina Ellwood stands, looking perfectly poised. The voices in the room haven't died down enough for me to hear all of it, but I'm able to catch the end.

"She has received many accolades and at such a young age. Please help me in welcoming a very talented violinist, Ms. Noelle Kennedy."

As everyone claps, a young woman steps to the front of the courtyard wearing a beautiful black strapless gown, with a violin propped to her chin. She holds the bow high and looks at the strings with her brows furrowed instead of looking at the crowd as if she's mustering up some inner strength. As soon as the bow hits the strings, music fills the courtyard like a rushing avalanche, and there is not one person that doesn't look affected by it.

"What do you say we get out of here?" Darren surprises me by whispering in my ear, and I look around to see Rausch has disappeared just as easily as he had appeared.

Darren's wearing a mischievous smile. "I thought you had to give a speech?" I ask.

"Not until later," he says. "Come on, there's something I want to show you."

With his hand barely on my elbow, I follow like a magnet being pulled through the crowd until we slip through one of the doors and enter a dimly lit hallway.

21

Emerson

Darren

We enter the hallway, leaving the sounds of violin music and the clinking of crystal glasses behind us.

"Are we allowed in here?" Evangeline asks, as I lead her down the dimly lit hall, passing closed exhibits.

"Don't tell me you weren't a rule-breaker in school," I say, raising my eyebrows at her.

The corner of her mouth tilts and she narrows her eyes at me in that sexy as fuck way when I annoy her... So I annoy her some more. "Or maybe you were a cheerleader?" I ask. "I'm liking the image of that."

Her eyes flare and I laugh as we take a turn down another hallway into an exhibit that I thought was the one I wanted, but it turns out not to be. Frustrated, I pull her down yet another dark hall, the sound of her heels echoing against the walls.

"Do you even know where you're going?" Evangeline asks breathlessly.

"Of course I do," I say, pulling her into another exhibit.

"I'm wearing heels, Darren." The exasperation in her voice is evident. "If this is a 10k charity walk, at least get me some gym shoes."

Stopping momentarily, I pin her with my eyes. "I will carry you over my shoulder all the way back to the atrium if I need to."

She shuts her mouth, the ruby red glistening in the soft lighting, but her eyes are still narrowed at me as if daring me to do it.

"You wouldn't."

"It would be my immense pleasure," I practically purr, and she swallows hard.

I pivot us into the entrance of the exhibit room and Evangeline stops short, because on the far wall is the photograph I wanted to show her.

She steps further into the room with trepidation until she's standing directly in front of it.

"I thought you might like a private viewing," I say a little nervously. I stand behind her, watching the rise and fall of her shoulders as she breathes in and out.

The tilt of her head causes fine pieces of hair to caress the side of her neck, and I want to run my finger over the arch, across her shoulder, and push the strap of her dress down so I can kiss the top of it, but I don't. Instead, I hold my breath, wondering what she's thinking, because her silence is killing me… and every moment she breathes instead of speaks causes a painful beat of my heart.

"It's Emerson," I say, stepping forward to stand next to her.

"I know," she says with a hint of humor.

"You don't like it?" I ask. "Because we can go back if you…"

"Shut up, Darren."

I do as I'm told, shoving my hands in my pockets and rocking back on my heels. She looks at the photograph as if she's memorizing every detail, and I find myself jealous of her attention to something other than me.

When I can't stand the silence anymore, I ask, "He's not a particularly good-looking gentleman is he?"

The profile accentuates his large nose and prominent chin. I realize I've never studied what Emerson looked like, only his words. But now, scrutinizing his picture, I can see why.

"It's not just about someone's physical appearance," she says without looking away from the photograph, "it's his words; what's in his heart, and how he lives his life," she continues. "I think he's kind of beautiful."

The way she talks about Emerson is hypnotizing – describing what's below skin and muscle to one's soul is the true meaning of beauty.

The piece of Emerson I used to hate belonged to my father – self-righteous and hypocritical. She strips away all the awful parts, allowing me to see a new version of him. Just as she threatens to make me fall in love with him, I begin to wonder.

"Who made you fall in love with Emerson?" I ask, and she finally turns to face me, her wide blue eyes filled with trepidation, and I feel as though my question has hit the vulnerable muscle between bone and tendon like the piercing of an arrow.

"Who says I'm in love with Emerson?" she asks, and it's not lost on me that she's evading my question, but I'm too distracted by the way her body moves and the red silk of her dress that leaves little to the imagination to keep hold of my thoughts.

"No love can be bound by oath or covenant to secure it against a higher love," I provide her with a particularly lovely quote by Emerson.

"Nobody talks like that anymore," she says, a romanticism in her eyes and her voice that makes me sad, because I've lost that innocence—or maybe I never had it to begin with—but I want a piece of it. I want to sink my teeth into it and shiver from its sweetness.

"It's a dead language, like Latin," I muse.

"Not dead. Just lost."

I sniff, loosening my bowtie and spinning around the room to look at all of the other framed photographs and paintings. "Have you ever had a client recite poetry to you in bed?" I ask. "Is that a kink?"

"That's a vulgar question."

"I'm a vulgar man."

She shakes her head and laughs, and it sounds like a thousand lit candles, throaty and bright. "But would that be so bad?" she asks, placing her hand on her hip. I focus on her nipples that draw tight and visible through the material of her dress, begging for me to run a thumb over the bud just to hear her suck in a breath.

"Do you know how badly I want to fuck you against Emerson's portrait?" I say in a low voice, unable to trust myself to move.

Her plump red lips tug into a smile. She blinks against her bangs, and when she parts her lips, my dick presses harder against the seam of my pants. She moves over to the photograph and stands in front of it. "This one?" she asks, pointing behind her, and I swear to fucking God, Emerson is looking right at me with judgmental eyes.

I stare back at her, willing myself not to move forward, because if I do, I won't be able to stop until I have her pinned against the wall, my hand cupping her cunt—I can almost guarantee her pussy will be so fucking wet I could slip two, maybe three fingers in so easily, and Jesus Christ, I'm torturing myself.

"You're tempting the devil, Evangeline," I practically growl, and she responds by tilting her head as she pushes the strap of her dress down her shoulder. Just a little bit more and I'd be able to see the dusky pink around her nipple. Lust unfurls deep in my belly, threatening to make me do things I know I shouldn't.

I palm my face because I can't look anymore, and when I close my eyes, the image of her standing in front of Emerson with her dress falling off her shoulder and tendrils of her hair brushing her neck is burned into my eyelids.

"Don't tell me you're not a rule-breaker, Darren Walker," she says, the sultry tone dripping from her lips, and my stomach tightens at the sound of her voice, at her words, at the fucking smell of her perfume mixed with the scent of her arousal that fills the small space between us.

When I drop my hand, she's in front of me like a tempting apple I want to take a bite of. How sweet it would taste.

"Or were you a Catholic schoolboy?" she asks, as she circles me, her hand on my shoulder, leaving embers trailing across my chest and back.

Her voice, her body, the promise hanging in the air, is fucking intoxicating. I breathe her in, lean into the heady air, charged and sweet, tilting my head to watch her move behind me, her lips close to my ear as I close my eyes. "If you want me, Darren," she whispers, "all you have to do is take me. Isn't that what you paid for?" My jaw tightens at her words.

I turn around so fast the room spins and take hold of her roughly, pulling her body into mine. She swallows at the feel of my erection pressing into her. My lips hover over hers as I look down, the pale blue of her eyes flashing, and I feel her hot breath on me, so *fucking* tempting.

She looks up at me through her long lashes just waiting, begging, and I want to give it to her, give her everything. She drives me fucking insane, and I don't care if we're in the National Portrait Museum and Emerson is fucking watching. Let him see me fuck her so hard she screams my name, waking every dead poet in this museum.

I grab hold of her neck and she sucks in a breath, making me groan.

Footsteps echo in the nearby hallway causing me to release her, and we leave the exhibit, racing down the opposite hallway towards the atrium while giggling.

22

I Don't Belong to You

Evangeline

"Where have you been?" Audrina asks as soon as we arrive safely back in the atrium, albeit out of breath. "Dinner's about to begin, and you still need to make your speech," she reminds him.

Darren's grip on mine loosens as his palm begins to sweat. The room spins with laughter and lights, clinking glasses, and soft music from a band that's set up behind the podium.

"Shit," he grumbles under his breath, trying to adjust himself as discreetly as he can.

I squeeze his hand reassuringly, and the look in his eyes is full of frustration and dizzying want. I have no doubt that Darren would have lifted the skirt of my dress, pushed my panties aside, maybe even ripped them off, so he could fuck me against the wall next to Emerson's portrait if we'd not been interrupted. My pulse still hasn't returned to normal from our hurried escape through the maze of hallways. The threat of being caught was an aphrodisiac that I can't quite seem to tamper down, even now while Audrina Ellsworth and her perfectly styled silver hair looks at Darren expectantly.

He loops his arm around my waist and pulls me to his side, giving me a chaste kiss on the cheek, but his lips linger for a few seconds longer than needed, feeling like a promise. The warmth of his jacket, the smell of his shampoo, and the tiny rapid pulse in his lips makes me reluctant to let him go.

"Save me," he whispers in my ear, which makes me giggle, all of my nervous energy expelled into his shoulder, and I grab onto him for support. Audrina clears her throat to get our attention and Darren pulls away.

Audrina doesn't seem to care about our inside joke. She stares right back at him, and he reluctantly lets go, my fingers slipping from his.

I stand at the outer perimeter of the room, having a good enough view while Audrina speaks into the microphone to get everyone's attention. The sound of her voice causes the room to hush as if a cloak's been thrown over the courtyard. When I look out at the guests, they're all turned towards the podium, and I can see Darren nervously playing with his cufflinks. He looks quite dashing in his tuxedo, the bowtie still loose around his neck.

"I'd like to introduce you to tonight's sponsor, Darren Walker," she says, and once she begins to clap, so does the rest of the room.

Darren clears his throat, and the clapping dies down to a slow patter of noise.

"As most of you know, the Abigail Pershing Foundation was created by my mother, Merrill Compton-Walker." There's a collective sigh at the mention of her name but

Darren continues. "It is," he falters, "*was*, a cause very dear to her, and she spent tireless hours raising money and awareness for domestic violence victims. As I look out at all of her friends and fellow patrons, I am proud of what she has accomplished, and I know that she is here with us tonight." Darren's voice cracks a tiny bit, and his public display of emotion is felt in the crowd. Rausch's words come back to haunt me: *And to think this is only scratching the surface of his potential.*

He makes a great effort to not live up to that potential, but does a very poor job at it. The way he stands at the podium with charming, nervous energy, and a smile that would rival the greatest politicians, I understand why Rausch and his father were so at odds with him.

He could do great things.

My pride is short lived when I feel a hand on my waist. "When I heard the news, I thought it was a joke," a familiar voice says close to my ear with a hint of amusement, "but here you are."

My nervous energy from earlier has come back with a vengeance. Senator Langley's blue eyes come into focus, and I realize now what Alistair meant about sharks wearing tuxedos – I just didn't realize that he was among them. I remember the last time I saw him, his fingers in my cunt under the restaurant table, his frustration at being interrupted by Senator Walker and his wife's tragic accident – how he was so willing to fuck me, even though his colleague and supposed friend had just died. It wasn't misplaced grief, it was indifference – a nuisance preventing him from satisfying an itch that he thought he was owed—an itch he'd been wanting to scratch for nearly four years, since the first time we'd met.

He stands close to me, his arm brushing against mine

as he looks out at the crowd. "You owe me something," he says in a low voice, full of innuendo.

Everyone is turned towards the podium where Darren stands, and his voice fades into background noise, overtaken by the static clouding my mind. I don't like feeling as if I'm not in control of a situation, but I try my best to stay calm, knowing that he wouldn't make a scene here.

"I think the statute of limitations is up," I retort and attempt to walk away, but his fingers dig painfully into my arm as he pulls me further away from the atrium and closer to an alcove hidden by potted trees and bushes.

"You'll fuck that little shit, Darren Walker, but not me?"

There was a time when I could handle a man like Jonathan Langley, a man who thinks he's entitled, but in this space, where I have never felt more out of place, I've lost my footing and my guard was down.

"I don't belong to you," I say while trying to shake him off, but his grip is iron clad.

I belong to Darren Walker, the man who paid five million dollars to fuck me on his father's desk, chase me through the hallways of his house naked, and sit on his grand piano with my legs spread for him.

I don't think Senator Langley cares about that. He only cares about what he's owed.

Darren appears, slicing the air between us and punching Senator Langley so hard I hear bone crack. My stomach turns and I lift my hands to cover my mouth.

"Keep your fucking hands off my *wife*!" Darren grits out, his chest heaving with anger and exertion.

I look back at the courtyard to see all eyes are on us.

The lapels of Darren's tux stretch across his chest as he breathes heavily. He takes my hand and I can feel it shake. I look down at Senator Langley, and oh God, what did

Darren do? But I don't have time to contemplate the weight of that answer because I'm being pulled toward the exit, my heart pounding against my chest. Once we're out of the courtyard, the lighting and the beautiful glass and steel structure of the atrium gone, replaced by drywall and muted colors – he stops and touches my face.

"I'm sorry," he whispers, lowering his forehead to mine, and I can feel his long lashes flutter against my cheeks. "I'm so sorry, I didn't think…" His hand is in my hair gripping tightly, pulling my low bun loose, and I can feel my hair fall around my shoulders, his fingers looping through the strands and gently tugging. The complicated hazel of his eyes searches mine. I don't know if he means he wasn't thinking when he brought me here, or he wasn't thinking when he punched Senator Langley.

Either way, there will be consequences.

Darren is a shameless playboy who drinks too much and cares too little for authority. But then he gives me a private tour of the museum to see Emerson's portrait, and then punches a US Senator for touching me.

"What was…"

I kiss him. I kiss him with all the anger and lust and shame bubbling up inside of me. It claws its way from somewhere deep in my belly and out through my fingers, which dig into his tuxedo jacket with frustration that it's not the lean muscles of his back. The question he was about to ask is long discarded when he kisses me back. It sears into me, claims me, and possesses me while he drags me into the coat check, shucking his jacket carelessly until we hit the wall at the back.

The air is knocked from my lungs, expelling a small gasp as his tall, lean frame threatens to melt me into the wall.

The rows of thick furs and expensive overcoats muffle our moans and sighs as we kiss, pawing at each other, pulling at clothes and skin.

I squirm under his touch as he lifts my dress to run his hand between legs, pushing my panties aside so he can feel how wet I am already. He groans into my mouth with satisfaction as I grind myself against his hand because I want more, and I want it now.

"*Queenie*," he says, and moves to nip and kiss me through my dress. He pushes the strap down exposing my breast and he breathes heavily, drunk on lust, drunk on power, as he kneads my soft flesh with his hand before he bites down on my nipple – the pain sears through like the push of a button, causing heat to flood at my center and I hiss through my teeth.

Shame floods my veins as I crave the possession, the need to be owned. I breathe into his mouth as his lips hover over mine, the corners tugging into a smile. I yank his belt free and pop the button of his dress pants while he tugs my panties down roughly, each of us fighting to get to a place where he can be inside me.

"Oh God," I pant the minute he pushes inside me, wide and deep without giving me a moment to adjust, and he's thrusting into me, causing my ass and back to hit the wall roughly as his hips move at a speed that is driven by the need to fuck – the need to *own*.

All the pent-up frustration and lust that was abandoned in the Emerson exhibit sags inside of me with relief at finally being satisfied.

I can feel his muscles work under the crisp, expensive fabric of his dress shirt as he turns me around, lifting my dress over my ass and driving back into me while my cheek and palms press against the wall. Short bursts of air brush against the back of my neck as he whispers how good I feel, how I belong to him—the word *mine* causing my orgasm to start to crest.

His fingers dig painfully into my hips, pushing and pulling until everything is tight like a band. He reaches around to cup my breasts and then moves his hand under the slit of my dress to circle my clit. My stomach begins to quiver, and I know I'm gone, past the point of no return, broken in half by the pain and the pleasure as the orgasm grips me like a snake, squeezing until there's nothing left to give, and the band breaks, sending me reeling.

The walls of my pussy grip his cock and he hisses, his thrusts shortening and the cadence slowing. He places a hand on the wall beside me, breathing heavily, his chest resting against my back, and I can feel the rapid beat of his heart as he sags against me. "You're *mine, Evan*," he rasps.

23
How a Bill Becomes a Law

Darren

"Goddammit, Darren!" Rausch shouts, his whole body shaking. Behind him is a half empty bookcase with law books leaning against each other, and a picture of him with my father when he was sworn in as Senator. The rest of the books are in boxes next to the desk.

"A fucking U.S. Senator!" he continues to yell, his cheeks turning red. "That's a federal offense!" He shakes his head while breathing heavily.

Rausch has always been an intimidating man, but only to someone who cares what he thinks – which I don't. Still, I can't help but jump a little bit in my seat at the rumble of his voice. Now that his king is gone, what will he do?

"He won't press charges," I say smugly.

"There were witnesses. It could be out of your hands." He throws his arms in the air but finally takes a seat at his desk, a pile of folders sits precariously at the edge, individual names written on each one.

"Are those candidates to replace my father?" I ask and narrow my eyes at the folders. Rausch scoops them up and tosses them to the side. My father's seat can't stay empty forever—Congress must go on—but I can't help but scoff.

"That's the governor's decision," I say, "until the term is up."

Rausch pierces me with a heavy stare. "I don't think you realize how long my reach can be."

I have no doubt Rausch has influence in many places.

"Answer me this," I begin and rest my forearms on the desk, "Rori Colton?" I laugh. "He took the Bar three times before he finally passed, and he's been arrested for a DUI!"

"Every politician has a skeleton in their closet. You've been around long enough to know that, and the public has a very short memory." He leans back in his chair with a satisfied smile. "And besides, at least he *took* the Bar, which is more than I can say for you," he fumes.

I've made it my life's mission to annoy the fuck out of him, and it doesn't matter if he doesn't recognize that as an accomplishment, because I sure as fuck do. The one thing that messed with my father's psyche the most was the fact that I went to law school but never took the Bar.

Rausch sits back in his chair and assesses me, which is unnerving. "If you were three years older, I'd back you for your fathers' seat."

I laugh, but his face remains stoic. "You're serious?

"You don't think I have confidence in you?"

"No. I think you want someone to manipulate like you did with my father."

Rausch laughs. "I don't think you knew your father at all."

"What's that supposed to mean?"

"Your father was stubborn, and once he had an idea to

do something, no one could stand in his way." Rausch adjusts the sleeves of his dress shirt. "If you think I was pulling the strings, you are mistaken."

"I'm not running for office," I say quickly, but I can't get over the fact that Rausch would actually have confidence in me to take office, even if it might be for his own benefit.

"Assaulting a U.S. Senator is not something that goes away easily," he starts again, just when I thought we had exhausted that subject. "Was it because of her?"

"You seem to know everything that goes on around Washington, so you tell me." Rausch wouldn't ask a question that he doesn't already know the answer to.

"She's a liability, Darren, a liability in a red dress, and in a town like this, everyone will know exactly what she is," Rausch glowers.

I wave him off. "Who do you think her clients were?"

"Jesus, Darren," he laments. "What the fuck am I supposed to do with that?"

"Was Langley…"

I stand up and place my hands on the desk while I look at him and say, "That *fuck,* Langley laid a hand on her, and you think it's her fault." I shake my head and laugh.

"She fucks men for money," he says in an unfeeling tone. "Do you want everyone to respect her just because she's your wife? If that's the case, you're even more naive than I gave you credit for," he laughs.

"She wouldn't have a profession if it weren't for men like Langley," I retort, "so don't lay the blame on her."

"Didn't you pay her for sex?" he asks, raising an eyebrow.

Shame sits heavy in my gut at the thought of it, but I don't have to explain myself to Rausch. I could say it was the coke and the whiskey, but I knew exactly what I was doing. Sometimes I feel as though I'm on autopilot to do the wrong thing.

I school my face to erase any emotion, sitting back down. "Does it even matter? I have no interest in being a politician," I remark.

"It seems politicians *and* lawyers are beneath you," he says, relaxing his jaw. "So tell me, is your noble profession to save girls with daddy issues? Because I'd say you're excelling." His patronizing tone causes me to grate my teeth.

"Maybe I'll get business cards printed," I snipe with an attitude.

Rausch lets out a frustrated breath of air and pinches the bridge of his nose. "What do you plan on doing with your life, Darren? Fucking that girl you call your *wife* will expire when the contract is up, and you'll have to find something else to occupy your time." His lips are pressed tightly together, waiting for my response.

My hand rests against my thigh, my pointer finger gently tapping against my pants to distract me. Through gritted teeth, I declare, "Not be a life-sucking lawyer, that's for sure."

Rausch laughs, causing his suit to wrinkle under the rumble of his chest.

"Do you know how hard it was for your father to sit back and watch you flush your life down the drain?" he asks, but I know he's not expecting an answer. "All the times he sent me to bail you out of jail or call in a favor, risking everything he built for you?" He gestures in my direction.

"You graduated from Yale to be a Senator's errand boy. Your parents must be so proud," I say defiantly.

"You graduated from Georgetown law, and you're sitting on the other side of this desk," he plants the pad of his finger against the dark grained wood, "so you don't get to make judgements about me. In fact, *Darren*, you can thank me for the fact that your inheritance tax isn't higher," he says with satisfaction, calling out the Bill my father helped pass in Congress.

I stare at him, making an unimpressed noise.

"Do you need me to sing the song *How A Bill Becomes a Law*?" he asks in a condescending tone, and I curse under my breath.

"If all your accomplishments are to make the rich richer, then I hope you sleep soundly at night while the other ninety-nine percent doesn't," I retort, realizing I sound a bit like Evangeline, worrying about the homeless. Jesus fuck, she's in my head.

Rausch laughs, his blue eyes lighting up with amusement. "He who sleeps in glass houses…" Rausch reaches into his desk and pulls out a manilla envelope, sliding it across the desk towards me.

"This is why you came, isn't it?" he asks.

I stare at the envelope and then back up at him without taking it. "What's this?"

"You did hold up your part of the bargain with the charity fundraiser," he nods. "I always follow through on my promises."

I steeple my fingers and press my lips to them before I move to take the envelope.

"Just know I take no delight in giving you this information."

24

You Taught Me Well

Evangeline

"How did you get this number?"

"Your grandmother gave it to me," my mother says, and I panic.

"Did something happen to her? Is she okay?" The director or one of the nurses at the facility would have called me if something had happened, but my nerves still feel frayed at the edges.

"No, no, she's fine," my mother explains, and my heart rate starts to return to normal.

I know the day will come when my grandmother is no longer here, but I'll never be ready for it. Multiple Sclerosis is a terrible disease, taking little pieces of the grandmother I used to know and turning her into someone who can no longer laugh, walk, or do the one thing she loved: sew.

"Then what do you want?" I ask, impatiently.

"You're my daughter, and I wanted to talk to you," she says with a hint of annoyance.

I can hear her breathe lightly into the phone, and I can

picture her with the same pale blue eyes and blonde hair, sitting at the kitchen table and looking out the back window – the one with chipped green paint – to the rusted swing set in the backyard.

It's my grandparents' property, a place I used to love until my grandfather died and my grandmother was diagnosed with MS. Everything changed after that. I suppose now it's mine, since I have power of attorney for my grandmother, but I haven't lived there for years.

She says softly, "It's good to hear your voice."

I let out a shaky breath and feel the chill of the fall air as someone enters the café, bringing with them a small gust of wind.

I want to believe that my mother is only calling to hear my voice because she misses me, but I know better.

"Did you happen to read the papers?"

"What papers? What are you talking about?" she asks, innocently.

She was never good at lying, at least not to me. "Are you still with him?" I demand, holding the phone tightly.

"Evangeline," she says with a sigh, "I wish you would just let things go."

My step-father is the reason we don't talk. "I have to go," I say, ready to pull the phone from my ear and hit the end button when she stops me.

"Wait, wait…"

I pause for a moment.

"Don't you think it's better if I handle things for Mimi?"

"Mimi is being well taken care of."

"By strangers," she scoffs.

"By trained professionals who know how to take care of her," I explain.

"They're not family," she argues. "She belongs with family. That place is bleeding her dry," my mother says, exasperated.

This isn't a new argument – it's one we've had ever since I had to put Mimi in the care home where professionals that know how to deal with MS can help her. My mother doesn't care so much that she's in a home, but that I have control over Mimi's money.

"Her money ran out a long time ago," I explain again, because she either doesn't believe me or doesn't remember. "I've been paying for her care." Her medication is expensive, not to mention the monthly cost of the care home.

"And we all know where that money comes from," she says with a condescending tone.

I regret having called her, but I regret ever telling her what I do for a living even more. At that moment when I did, I wasn't in a good place. I needed a mother to tell me I didn't have to fuck men for money, that she would find another way to help take care of Mimi… but she didn't. Instead, she told me maybe if I was lucky, I'd marry a rich client.

Hot tears burn in the back of my eyes. Maybe this is why I understand how Darren feels, because no matter how much we act out or pretend that it doesn't bother us, all we want is to be loved and accepted for who we are by our parents.

I'm on the verge of openly crying in this café, and I will not let her… I will not *allow* her to cause me any more pain. My coffee is lukewarm, so I push it away.

"Never stopped you from taking it," I accuse.

"I didn't call to argue with you."

"So why did you call? Because I know it's not about Mimi."

She breathes softly into the phone, and I try to picture her as the person she was when I was little.

"It's been a tough couple of months," she admits, and her voice sounds small. I have no doubt she's had it rough, but just like I do, she has to live with her choices too.

"If it has something to do with the house, just send me the bill." As long as my grandmother is alive, I won't let her house fall to ruin, but I know better than to give money to my mother.

"I see you did good for yourself though," she says, showing her cards. "Finally got a rich client to marry you." Her voice is resentful, and it sends a chill up my spine that I have to shake off.

I suck in a shaky breath. "You taught me well," I say, before hanging up the phone.

25

The Perfect Fuck You

Darren

I take the subway from the Capitol Building into Georgetown where I only have to walk a block in the chilly late afternoon to *The Tombs*, a bar I started hanging out at when I went to college. The neighborhood looks the same, and when I reach the familiar beige brick building with green awnings, I can already hear the ruckus inside as someone exits through the heavy wood doors.

Everything about this bar screams nostalgia, and not just my own. Lining the brick walls are framed photos of twentieth century propaganda. It's a Georgetown staple, and I find Alistair in one of the booths in the back, his back to the wall with his long legs stretched out over the red leather seat. He's wearing sunglasses and a tie that's pulled loose. I shake my head and walk over to the booth, kicking his feet off before sliding into the opposite side.

"Rough night?" I ask, while Alistair pulls the shades from his face and sets them down on the table between us.

He's already taken the liberty of ordering shots, but it looks like he didn't wait for me to arrive.

"More like a rough day," he groans.

"Aww, did you have to roll out of bed before noon?" I signal the waitress to bring another round.

"Har, har," Alistair says, pointing his finger in the air dramatically. "I'll have you know that you are looking at the employed," he says with a proud grin.

"Who are you, and what have you done with my eternally lazy and depraved friend, Alistair?" I joke.

"I assure you, it's still me under this dress shirt and tie," he jokes back.

"Something tells me I want you to be sober—well, mostly sober—when you explain this job you're talking about. Which, by the way, I hope is legal."

He scoffs. "Of course it's legal. Capital Management." Alistair leans forward, placing his elbows on the table. "Did you know people have to be at work by nine a.m?" he asks.

"Yes," I laugh. "What exactly do you do?" I ask, trying to figure out what the hell he's talking about.

"I'm still figuring that out," he laughs, and then raises his shot glass.

"To…" Alistair pauses as if he's trying to think of something witty to toast. "To capital management, whatever the fuck that is!"

I toss back my shot and suck in a breath. Alistair sets his empty glass back down with a thud.

He scratches his head and then levels me with a mostly serious gaze. "My dad's friend runs this investment firm, and, well…." He leaves the sentence unfinished, looking sheepish, and I understand why.

We'd had a pact to be nothing like our fathers, and here he is, working at a firm his father set up for him.

"I'm happy for you."

Alistair shifts uncomfortably in his seat.

"You're all grown up," I tease to break the tension.

"He threatened to cut me off if I didn't at least try."

"I guess I'll have to find someone else to be a degenerate with."

"You wouldn't dare," he sounds wounded.

"Of course not. I'm not that kind of asshole."

"Speaking of assholes," Alistair says with a sober look, "how did it go with Rausch?"

"Same old, same old. What are you going to do with your life? Giving me shit about not taking the Bar, blah, blah."

"Remind me again why you *didn't* take the Bar?" he asks.

I roll my eyes and lean back in my seat. I could have taken the Bar right out of law school. There was a job waiting for me at a local firm but… "The thought of trading in my freedom for a suit and jacket wasn't appealing," I admit out loud to Alistair. "No offense," I say pointing to his loosened tie.

"None taken," he says, tipping one of the shots back. "It's not so bad." He leans forward against the table. "Did you know there's sick days and vacation days?" He raises a teasing eyebrow.

"You've only been there one day," I point out.

"And I made a very good first impression."

I chuckle. "I have no doubt."

The bar starts to fill up as people clock out of work, and college students because of the proximity to Georgetown University. A group of friends take the table nearby, singing a fraternity drinking chant, and I turn to Alistair.

"Did we look as ridiculous as them?" I ask, tilting my head towards the group again, and thinking about how simple things were for me back then.

"Worse," Alistair teases.

"Did you get any information out of him about your grandfather?"

I lay the manilla envelope onto the table with an ominous thud.

"I take it you haven't read it?" The strings are still looped tightly.

"I read it. Most of it I already knew, but there was a police report for a Gregory Allen Walker from Lynchburg, Virginia, arrested on charges of arson."

Alistair gives me a concerned look.

"If Rausch thinks this is sufficient," I flip the corner of the envelope in frustration, and leave the sentence hanging, "he's fucking with me."

I don't mention the envelope with Evangeline's name on it, because I haven't looked at that yet. There can't be anything in there that I don't already know. I'd already had her checked out before I had the marriage contract drawn up. I was desperate, but I wasn't an idiot. No known arrests, no rehabs, nothing criminal. A simple credit check revealed some student loans that had been paid off, nothing of interest. Whatever Rausch put in that envelope, I either already know, or I don't want to know.

"Maybe he's just giving enough information so you can draw your own conclusions," Alistair shrugs.

That's probably the only smart thing Alistair has said tonight, because on the police report is an address. Granted, the police report is from over thirty years ago.

"Punching Senator Langley saved the evening from becoming boring," he chuckles, changing the subject. "So I guess forking over a hefty donation wasn't for nothing," he shrugs.

"Felt pretty good too," I add.

"What about Evangeline?" Alistair asks lightly.

My eyes snap up to his. "What about her?"

"It was over her, right?"

I nod, not going into detail.

"So what does that mean?" Alistair probes.

"What do you mean, what does that mean?" I demand, pulling a face.

Alistair shrugs with a smile. "You hired her so you could get control of your parents' estate."

I hold my hands up. "Don't try to be witty, Alistair. Just say whatever the fuck you want to say."

"You punched a U.S. senator over her." Alistair laughs, smacking his palms on the table with a loud thud, causing the empty shot glasses to clink together.

I breathe heavily, feeling that same anger that sliced through me the night of the charity dinner while I stood at that podium speaking in front of D.C.'s most prominent. I watched as he dug his fingers into her arm and the look on her face was what made me leave the podium and stalk through the crowd.

She looked scared, and I didn't like it.

"He fucking *touched* what's *mine*!" I raise my voice.

The table next to us stops talking and stares in our direction. Alistair bursts into laughter, pulling my attention back to him.

"What is so fucking funny?" I ask, incredulously.

"Oh God, Dare," he continues to laugh. "I have known you for a very long time."

"Preschool," I offer.

"Do you remember Taylor Burrell?" Alistair asks, raising an eyebrow.

"Yeah," I answer suspiciously.

"You dated her for six months, and you didn't even care when she left the Zeta Psi Halloween party with that asshole, Danny Flay," Alistair explains.

"He was a shitty midfielder." I shake my head. "Look, don't make more out of this than it is."

"Fine, fine," Alistair concedes. "I just hope you know what you're doing." He shakes his head again.

I motion for the waitress to bring more shots when Alistair stops me. "I gotta get going." He looks at his watch. "*Caroline* and *Remington,*" he says his parents' first names with a purposeful, pretentious undertone, "are hosting a dinner." He rolls his eyes, and the mention of his parents causes my chest to tighten. It must show in my eyes because Alistair suddenly looks apologetic.

"You know you're always welcome," he offers. "Caroline likes you better anyway," he jokes.

"Nah, I gotta get going," I say, reaching into my pocket and throwing a few bills onto the table. "Give Caroline and Remington my best."

Tucking the envelope back in my jacket, I take the stairs up to the street level and realize it's been raining, so I give Bailey a call to pick me up. It's a short ride back to the house, even with the inclement weather holding up traffic. The sound of rain hitting the roof of the sedan is oddly satisfying, and I don't realize we're at the house until the car comes to a stop.

"Thanks, Bailey," I say, and stop him before he gets out of the car with an umbrella. "No need."

"Have a good night, Mr. Walker," Bailey replies.

I'm not used to being called Mr. Walker, especially by Bailey who was my father's driver. I can tell in the tone of his voice that it feels odd for him too, but I exit the car without saying anything, and Bailey pulls away from the curb.

The rain is coming down good now, and I jog up the walkway, splashing puddles in my wake, and take the steps two at a time. Everything is dark and cold when I enter, no sound or smell of coffee coming from the kitchen, and when I get to the stairs, there's no light coming from the guest room where Evangeline has been staying.

I hold onto the railing for a moment longer before deciding to go into my father's office.

As I sit down behind the desk, my hair still wet from the walk up to the house, tiny drops of rain fall from my hair and hit the manilla envelope in front of me. My curiosity has gotten the better of me. Either that, or Alistair is in my head about caring too much about a girl I paid five-million dollars to be my wife.

I empty the contents of the envelope marked Evangeline across my father's desk.

My heart skips a beat, my breath shallow and empty like a cavern.

I think about finding Evangeline here shortly after we came back from Vegas. The way her fingers pressed against the spines of the books as if she'd been trying to figure out which one she wanted to read first, or maybe revisiting an old favorite. The sight of her in here was arresting, the oversized t-shirt just barely covering her ass, and the thought of fucking her on my father's desk was overwhelming and intoxicating; the perfect *fuck you*.

But I guess the *fuck you* was on me.

My eyes shift over to the framed Emerson poem on the wall behind me and my heart beats faster, my veins unable to hold the sudden surge of blood flow. I could never understand the love my father had for Emerson, but hearing Evangeline describe the meaning behind the lines – the way her cheeks flushed pink, and her pale blue eyes seemed to gleam like the ocean in sunlight – made me want to understand more. Maybe I always knew but refused to let myself think of the possibility, because even though I didn't get along with my father, I always held him to a higher standard, one that I could never reach so I never tried, but, of course he was human, and humans are flawed.

I can hear footsteps in the hall, the sound of wet sneakers on the wood flooring.

When I look up, I see her standing in the doorway, her eyes trained on the photos spread out before me: photos of her and my father. As if I'd made a noise – and maybe I did – her eyes snap up to mine, and even if I hadn't had the proof right in front of me, her eyes are like a door leading to the dark place where she keeps all of her secrets.

How could I have been so stupid?

At the museum, I had asked her who made her fall in love with Emerson, and she avoided answering the question.

As if a puzzle piece fits into place, it all makes sense now.

Evangeline knew my father.
She knew him before we ever met.

Continue the Kingmaker Trilogy with Queen of Ruin, book 2.

Read on for an excerpt of Queen of Ruin.

QUEEN OF RUIN EXCERPT
DARREN

"If this is where you go to escape, then I'm seriously worried about you." I hear Alistair's voice say from behind me, and when I turn to look at him, he's wearing a lopsided smile with his hands shoved into the pockets of his grey wool overcoat.

"Do you remember coming here on our elementary school field trip?" I ask him, as he walks up the steps to meet me.

"Of course," he says.

We both stare at the Lincoln Memorial, nineteen feet of carved marble, Lincoln's expression making him look like a formidable force, with his left hand clenching the arm of the chair he sits upon. It is an impressive feat of what man's hands can accomplish when put to the use of good; a symbol that even a country torn apart by war can come together and create something beautiful.

"Did you know that Lincoln is carved from twenty-eight pieces of Georgia Marble?" I ask.

"I was too busy chasing Poppy McBride around the

columns to pay attention to our tour guide," Alistair chuckles lightly.

"Why does that not surprise me?" I smile.

"Because you know me too well."

"There is a lot of information the tour guides don't tell you about the Lincoln Memorial. For instance, one of the workers must have grabbed the wrong stencil and chiseled an E instead of an F for Future in the Inaugural speech," I say. "They filled it in with concrete, but you can still see the flaw if you look hard enough."

"I guess I didn't miss as much as I thought," Alistair says, propping his foot on the step above.

"Something else interesting they don't tell is the dedication ceremony was racially segregated," I laugh cynically.

"That's fucked up, but why are we here, Darren?"

"Revisionist history, Alistair," I say, pointing my finger in the air and then taking a seat on the step.

It's a particularly lovely day in Washington D.C. with only a few clouds dotting the sky, the sun lighting up the lawn and making the grass look like a sea of emerald, yet there is a chill in the air, a sign of winter on the horizon when snow will cover the city, causing the branches of the white oak trees bow.

Alistair takes a seat next to me, stretching out his long legs over the marble steps.

"We look back on history and memorialize a great man, making him almost inhuman, God-like, a pillar of freedom representing everything we thought this nation was built on, but we forget about the flaws. We minimize them because we want to see him as a great man. His martyrdom makes it impossible to point them out. It's true, Lincoln had one foot in the twentieth century, but the other foot was still planted heavily in nineteenth," I lecture, "and yet, here we sit on the steps of this memorial, and I cannot help but internalize all of that hope for a better future."

"We're not really talking about Lincoln, are we?" Alistair asks.

"I didn't get along with my father," I say as a matter of fact. "That's never been in question; it's been a constant since as far back as I can remember," I sigh, tilting my head towards Alistair who looks down at his clasped hands. "But I thought I knew him."

"Anything in particular that you didn't know?" he asks.

I pull out the envelope and hand it to Alistair. He takes it with questioning eyes and then pulls it open, peering inside.

"Fuck," he says, closing the envelope as if to keep the secrets from making their way out.

I take the envelope and stuff it back into the inside pocket of my jacket.

I lean my forearms on my thighs and run my hands through my hair as I bow my head. The cold marble seeps through my jeans, causing a chill to run along my spine, goosebumps forming along my arms and legs.

"Who gave those to you?" Alistair asks, breaking through my thoughts, and I raise an eyebrow at him. "Ah, let me guess, Rausch?" He gives a dark laugh.

"He wants to drive a wedge between me and Evangeline," I state resolutely.

I only just now realized that, having time to clear my mind and think. Rausch didn't do this with a generous heart to warn me of Evangeline's history, but in doing so, he was willing to tarnish my father's reputation, at least in my eyes. Rausch is not the type of man who does anything by chance, but rather like a chess player, always looking three moves ahead.

"I know he's pissed that you circumvented the will, but now that it's done, what does it matter to him?"

"Other than to gloat that he was right about marrying her?" I scoff.

"If the press had gotten ahold of them…" Alistair doesn't finish his sentence, but he doesn't have to. This would be a huge scandal. Politics runs on perception, and just the mere accusation of my father being unfaithful, or better yet, taking advantage of a young college student because of his status, would be enough to ruin him.

"Someone's had these for four years, Alistair," I say, my voice sounding gravelly with the weight of it. "I have a feeling I know who it is."

Read Queen of Ruin, book 2 in the Kingmaker Trilogy.

ALSO BY PAULA DOMBROWIAK

THE BLOOD & BONE SERIES

A Steamy Rockstar Romance series

BLOOD AND BONE (BOOK 1)

Two days. One Interview. Twenty-five years of Rock 'n Roll. Telling his story might just repair past relationships and ignite new ones.

BREATH TO BEAR (BOOK 2)

These chains that weigh me down, my guilt I wear like a crown, SHE is my Breath to Bear

BONDS WE BREAK (BOOK 3)

To have and to hold from this day forward - to love and to cherish, till death do us part - and these are the bonds we break.

BOUND TO BURN (BOOK 4)

Love has a way of blazing through you like poison, leaving you breathless but still wanting more.

BLOOD & BONE BOXSET PLUS BONUS NOVELLA

All four books in the Blood & Bone series plus a bonus novella.

Blood & Bone legacy, bonus novella, give you a glimpse twenty years in the future through the eyes of their children.

This is their legacy.

Already read the series but just want the bonus novella?

Grab it exclusively on my SHOP

BLOOD & BONE LEGACY, A BONUS NOVELLA

STANDALONES

BEAUTIFUL LIES

I own the boardroom. He owns the stage. We were never meant to be together, but when somethings forbidden, it only makes you want it more.

A forbidden, reverse age gap romance

KINGMAKER SERIES

A Steamy, Marriage of Convenience, Political Romance Trilogy

KING OF NOTHING, BOOK 1 - March 12, 2024

QUEEN OF RUIN, BOOK 2 - June 11, 2024

STATE OF UNION, BOOK 3 - September 10, 2024

ABOUT THE AUTHOR

Paula Dombrowiak grew up in the suburbs of Chicago, Illinois but currently lives in Arizona. She is the author of Blood and Bone, her first adult romance novel which combines her love of music and imperfect relationships. Paula is a lifelong music junkie, whose wardrobe consists of band T-shirts and leggings which are perpetually covered in pet hair. She is a sucker for a redeemable villain, bad boys and the tragically flawed. Music is what inspires her storytelling.

If you would like a place to discuss Paula's books, you can join her Facebook Reader Group **Paula's Rock Stars Reader Group**

You can always find out more information about Paula and her books on her website

PAULADOMBROWIAK.COM

You can also purchase eBooks, signed paperbacks, audiobooks, and multi-book bundles on her direct shop.

payhip.com / PaulaDombrowiakBooks

ACKNOWLEDGMENTS

I could not have written this book without the support of my family. Thank you so much for always being there for me, and for allowing me the space to create.

To my beautiful alpha reader's, Nattie (a.k.a. Poopsie) and Mishie, I wouldn't be who I am without your friendship and this book would not be possible without your support and incredible feedback. I'm not sure how I got so lucky to call you both friends but you're stuck with me for life.

Lucy, you wonderful human being you. Thank you for being my friend and my supporter. You are and always will be my little metal head.

To my editor Dayna Hart, what a wonderful job you did with this book, cleaning up messes and making it into something readable.

Thank you to Katy Nielsen for proofreading. You are and always will be the one to find and fix all my errors, especially homophones. I may leave a few in there for you on purpose, just to keep you on your toes.

To my street team, the Rockettes (although we should rename it to the Jaxson Human fan club), you know who you are. Thank you for sharing all my teasers on your social media because it makes a huge difference for this little indie author. Thank you for your friendship, and the laughs. I love you girls!!!

To all the Bookstagrammers, Bloggers, and Booktokers

out there who have supported me, shared my posts, reviewed my books, and reached out to me, thank you, thank you, thank you! Word of mouth is huge! Your love of books astounds me, and I am so grateful to be a part of such a wonderful book community.

To my ARC readers, thank you from the bottom of my heart for reading and providing your honest review. Reviews are so important - especially for us little indie authors.

Last, but certainly not least, to my readers!!! I can't tell you how much you mean to me. In my heart I've always been a writer, but you make it real. I am always touched when readers reach out to me to say how much they connected with my characters. I strive to write from the heart, create characters that are real and flawed, and portray them in the most sensitive way possible. I hope you continue on this journey with me. Thank you for your support!

Printed in Great Britain
by Amazon